Dogs Don't Lie

A Kallie Collins Cozy Mystery Novel

Book One

Lisa Shay

ISBN: 9781686589409

Chapter 1

My palms started to sweat as soon as I turned the corner and saw cars packed in the driveway and lining both sides of the street in front of my parents' house. I didn't need to be a detective to know this wasn't the casual family dinner my mom led me to believe. Leaning against the hood of my truck and using my best John McClane Die Hard impersonation, I whispered, "Come over to the house, we'll get together, have a few laughs."

Pushing upright, I muttered under my breath, "Right, Mom."

I bit at my lower lip and frowned. I'm not comfortable with large groups of people I barely know. Honestly, sometimes not with small ones either.

Laughter followed a wisp of smoke drifting over the tall cedar fence separating the front and back yards. The tantalizing aroma of grilled meat meant Dad had the barbeque fired up and my stomach growled in anticipation. Resistance was futile.

Gathering resolve, I stopped on the top step at the front door. I glanced down at my faded blue Wranglers and worn not-so-white Skechers. I also didn't need to be a psychic to know Mom would voice her opinion of my wardrobe choices.

The minute I walked through the door, I knew I was right.

Meeting me in the foyer, Mom's over-the-top smile faltered just for a flash before the twinkle returned to her blue eyes. She smoothed the waist of her teal-and-purple sweater that went perfectly with her turquoise pants. Impeccable as always, not a single blond hair was out of place. "Kallie, honey, come in. Everyone's out back."

"Yeah, I saw that. There's quite the parking lot out front. You didn't tell me all your friends and half the neighborhood would be here. What's going on?"

"Sweetheart, can't I invite my beautiful, talented daughter to dinner and show her off without you questioning my motives? Not everyone has a doctor in the family."

"A veterinarian, Mom." I smiled. "You need to be clear on that. When people find out, they react"—I grimaced—"like they're startled."

Waving her hand, Mom dismissed the issue. She ushered me into the bright, airy kitchen and turned me to face her. Hands on my shoulders, she eyed me up and down. "Why must you always dress like …" Her tongue clicked out a disapproving tempo. She tugged at the sleeve of my Star Wars T-shirt. "What happened to that lovely green top I got you last week? It went so well with your hair." She sighed. "And jeans. Must you always wear jeans and dirty tennis shoes? I bought you such precious outfits growing up." Her voice quieted. "Enough said." Taking my arm, she tried to aim me toward the patio.

Resisting her, I didn't budge. "Mom, I'm on call starting in …" I glanced at the Mickey Mouse watch on my wrist. "Two hours." I smiled and lifted my hands. "I couldn't exactly pull a calf or stitch up a horse that ran through a fence in a precious outfit."

"At least let me do something with your hair." Mom stepped behind me and pulled at the black scrunchie, freeing my ponytail. She ran her fingers through to the ends, fluffing the long strands. In a wistful tone so full of love, she said, "You inherited your grandmother's hair—all red and curly."

Even standing behind me, I could feel her smile. "I know, Mom. But I also got her freckles."

"Angel kisses," she sang. "You got your father's eyes, though. That dark blue—sparkly and bright, like a sapphire."

"You're stalling." Spinning around to face her, my arms crossed, I took in a deep breath and let it out in a long sigh. "Come clean. You've set me up again, haven't you?"

She shrugged and looked away. "We thought it would be nice to have a barbeque with a few of the neighbors." Meeting my gaze, she said, "Okay. Yes. It's Lynn's nephew. He's visiting from Eugene. Since you and Eddie are about the same age, I said I'd invite you." In that sing-song voice she added, "Perfectly harmless."

"A few of the neighbors?" I glanced at her sideways and chuckled.

Smiling, her eyes wide, she feigned innocence. "Just our *closest* friends."

Laughing, I asked, "Is Dani here?" My married and pregnant-with-her-second-child younger sister often acts as my advocate in these situations, championing my life path. Mom means well, but sometimes she just has trouble acknowledging Dani and I are very different people.

"One of Katie's little friends from preschool had a birthday party this afternoon. Danielle said they'd stop by after." Mom gestured toward the patio.

Glancing outside, I nodded, biting my lower lip. "Fine. I'll meet him." I only had to stay a couple hours before I'd need to leave, check in at work, and get a company truck. *I can do this.*

"I think you'll like him. You should have lots to talk about. He recently passed the bar."

"A lawyer? What could we possibly have to—"

Before I could finish my protest, she placed her hand on my lower back and propelled me out the open French doors and onto the sunny brick patio. "Just go meet him. You never know."

"Hey, sweetie. Glad you could come," Dad called, one hand holding a spatula and the other waving away a sudden blast of smoke from the grill.

Tilting my head, I wiggled my fingers in his direction. "Thanks, Dad."

Lynn rushed Eddie over. He had that same deer-in-the-headlights look I knew I did. And even though he wasn't wearing a suit and tie right then, he might as well have been. I could see it in his manner, the way he carried himself—all businesslike and stiff.

"Hi, Kellie."

"Hi, Eddie. And it's Kallie."

"Oh. Sorry." He nodded. "Kallie. That's pretty."

"Thanks." The awkward general niceties out of the way, I searched my blank mind for something to say while checking for an opening in the tall cedar fence, or an unlatched gate. No such luck.

"Lynn, could you help me with the salads?" Mom and her buddy slipped away on false pretenses, leaving Eddie and me alone.

"So you're a doctor." He gestured with his beer bottle in my general direction.

My smile vacillated between a grin and grimace. "Yeah. I'm a vet."

"Cool." He tipped his head. "Good. Well, thank you for your service."

I almost laughed. "No. Not that kind. A veterinarian—an animal doctor."

Face wrinkling, he took a step back. "Animals?"

Mom had done it again. "Yes. Dogs, cats, horses, sheep, cows." I shrugged one shoulder. "Whatever."

"That must be, umm … interesting." He took a long drink and scanned the backyard. It was his turn to look for an opening to retreat.

I recognized the panic in his eyes. I'd seen that look before. Eddie needed an out, freeing both of us from this disaster. My voice raised in excitement and I nodded with enthusiasm. "Yes, it is. Last week I pulled a calf from a heifer. Let me tell you, she was not happy. I had my arm inside her—"

"Whoa," Eddie cried. He held up a hand and scowled. "TMI."

Lynn appeared balancing three bags of chips atop a large bowl of potato salad.

Eddie saw his escape. "Aunt Lynn, let me help you." With a momentary glance in my direction, he murmured a terse, "Excuse me." He hurried over, took the bowl from her, and walked toward the long table set up on the freshly mowed lawn—away from me.

"Works every time," I mumbled. With an overwhelming sense of relief, I relaxed and headed to the grill. "Hey, Dad. Could you cook me a burger to go?"

He frowned. "Why don't you stay? Eat with us. Dani will be here later."

My phone vibrated, alerting me to an incoming text. I pulled it from my hip pocket and glanced at the screen. Work summoned. "Sorry. Gotta go. Duty calls." I think my attempt at not sounding *too* cheerful failed.

Dad pulled a bun from a large pack, tossed it on a paper plate, and handed it to me. "I'll have your burger ready in a minute—to go."

I stood on tiptoes and kissed his smooth cheek. "Thanks, Dad."

⊙⊙

Holding my burger and shifting with one hand, steering wheel in the other, I drove the ten miles to the Crater Emergency Animal Hospital. Moaning with pleasure, I stuffed the last smoky, cheesy, barbequey bite into my mouth and killed the engine. The driver's door of my beat-up old truck squeaked as I opened it and squealed in protest when I slammed it shut. Wiping my lips with the back of my hand and brushing crumbs from my jeans, I pushed through the front entrance's double doors.

The empty waiting area was quiet except for the canned music. Glancing down the long hall, I noticed that all the exam room doors were open. I slowed, stopping at the front desk. "Eric, what's up?"

Looking at me over the tall counter, he held up one finger, furiously chewing a bite of his sandwich. He swallowed. "Sorry to bother you. I know you're not officially on until five, but Sanders just left for a call in Prospect. It'll take him almost an hour just to get there." He ripped a sheet off the pink message pad, handing it to me. "This sounds urgent."

I frowned. "Yeah. Okay. What—"

"Just read it. It's all I got. Detective B. Jacobson didn't go into much detail." He shook his head, his eyebrows rising.

I looked at the note.

Jackson County Sheriff's Department, requesting a vet. ASAP.
See Det. B. Jacobson at scene.

An address followed. "Eagle Point." I glanced up at Eric. "Is an animal injured? Why are the police involved?"

"Don't know. They're requesting assistance. A-S-A-P. And like I said, that's all I got." The phone rang and Eric picked it up. "Crater Emergency Animal Hospital."

I hurried down the hall to the back of the large building, grabbed a key hanging from a peg at the rear door, and pushed out into the parking lot. After unlocking a company truck, complete with everything I'd need in the utility bed to care for an injured or sick animal, I climbed inside and programmed the address into the GPS.

Twenty minutes later, after the "your destination is on the right" and "arrived" prompts from the sultry female GPS voice, I turned onto a long gravel driveway.

One green-and-white sheriff's vehicle, a shiny black unmarked Dodge Charger, and a dark-blue Oregon State Police cruiser, engines quiet and emergency lights off, sat parked just outside a well-kept two-story farmhouse.

A deputy sheriff hurried over to my truck, his hand up to stop me.

I rolled my window down, hoping I wouldn't need to go into a lengthy explanation. Holding the pink note ready, I opened my mouth. But before I could say anything—

"I'm sorry, miss. You're going to have to leave." The deputy motioned for me to turn around. Then he did a double take, his eyes stopping on the utility bed of my truck. "Wait. Are you the vet?"

"Yes." I nodded, waving the pink note out the window. "I'm Dr. Collins. I'm supposed to meet with Detective Jacobson."

"Glad you're here. Ben's getting impatient. Park over there." He pointed next to the sheriff's vehicle. "I'll let him know you're here, Dr. Collins." Keying the mic attached to his shoulder epaulet, he turned away.

"Impatient?" I frowned, butterflies fluttering in my stomach. "That doesn't sound good. Hope I'm in time." I parked and switched off the engine.

"Come on. I'll take you to Ben."

Scrambling out of the truck, I ran to catch him. The butterflies abandoned their fluttering for somersaults, and I burped barbeque. Good thing I'd popped a breath mint on the way. "Wait. What do I need? Is there an injured animal or … what exactly?"

Glancing back at me, he gestured to the barn. "Ben will explain everything to you."

He led me past the house and through the long breezeway. Warm air swept inside, stirring the scent of damp earth, fresh hay, and that sweet, musky aroma of horses. My pulse ramped up, pounding in my ears. I'd graduated in the top ten of my class and was going on six months in practice, and even when I knew what I was walking into, the thought of a sick or injured animal made me nervous. I guess that's a good thing. A life counted on me to make the right decisions. I took a deep breath, held it for a beat, and then released the air through pursed lips. *Give me wisdom and guidance, Lord.*

We continued beyond an open gate into a grassy field fenced by green five-foot-tall T-posts, three feet of woven wire, and a double strand of barbed wire on top. Halfway inside the field, maybe a hundred yards from me, a man in a dark-gray suit stood about twenty-five feet from a massive old oak tree. I squinted, searching for the form of a horse or cow lying in the grass. Nothing. *Could this be some kind of drive-by shooting? Of animals?* Possibilities flashed. My heart skipped with dread at what might await me.

Approaching the man, Detective B. Jacobson I presumed, I spotted a small brown lump in the grass under the tree. Well, it was small compared to a cow or horse. At the far end, another sheriff's deputy, a woman, and the state patrolman walked the edge of the fence.

"Hey, Ben. The doc's here."

Without turning, Detective Jacobson responded, "Thanks, Brent. Could you go back out front and wait for the CSU? Show them in?"

"Sure thing, Ben." Brent tipped his head as he passed me. "If there's anything I can do, Doc, tell Ben. He can radio me."

I managed a weak smile. "Thanks."

Detective Jacobson turned, his serious expression slipping. Mouth open, he straightened, his crossed arms dropping to his sides. "Oh." He shook his head. "I'm sorry. I wasn't expecting someone ..." He rubbed his forehead. "I'm sorry. I guess I expected someone older."

So had I. I had more of a Columbo type pictured, not this young man. "And maybe someone with a Y chromosome." I chuckled.

His face reddened and he smiled, creating dimples in his cheeks. He slipped off his sunglasses, revealing piercing green eyes. "No. Nooo ..." He sighed. "Okay. Maybe. Again. I am sorry." He held out his hand. "I'm Detective Jacobson. Thank you for coming so quickly."

He really was trying to apologize. That it embarrassed him was, well, kinda cute. "I'm Doctor Collins." I stepped forward and took his offered hand, but the shake was fleeting. I looked toward the furry form under the tree. Glancing back at the detective, I grinned. "At least you didn't work 'little lady' into your apology."

"Ouch." His eyes narrowed. "Have people actually said that to you?"

"Oh, yes. More than you would imagine." I walked past him, toward what I then saw was a big dog—lots of long brown, tan and black fur, floppy ears twitching whenever a fly tickled. He looked uninjured, eyes bright and alert. His head rested on something long and whitish-brown held under enormous paws.

"I wouldn't get too close."

Ignoring his warning, I stopped about ten feet away and knelt. "Hi, buddy. What's up?"

His tail thumped the ground, churning up a small dust storm.

"Whatcha got there? Can I see?" I crept a little closer.

"It's a bone. We suspect human. Every time we get near, he growls— shows his teeth. The people who live here don't know who the dog belongs to. I ... well, I thought maybe if you had a tranq gun—I'd hate to have to shoot him."

I jumped up and spun toward him. "You were going to shoot him?"

He held up his hands. "Like I said, I don't want to, but I need that bone."

"He doesn't need to be shot ... *or* drugged." I relaxed. "Just give me a minute."

He backed away, nodding. "Please. Take your time."

Kneeling again, I sat cross-legged in the grass. My thoughts quieted, and I tuned out the soft voices of the two officers across the field. Taking in a deep breath, I looked at the dog. "Where, buddy?" Images played in my mind. *The bone under his paws. Fresh churned earth. More bones protruding from dark soil.*

From the dog, answers in the form of images and sensations raced into my mind. Pictures flashed. *Warm sunshine. Insects buzzing. Sweet grass. The scent of fresh turned soil. Another field. Not here, but close. Cool water running in a ditch, eroding an area. Bones—a human skull.*

"Okay," I whispered and envisioned more of my own images. *Him giving me the bone. Scratching behind his ears. Me following him to the other bones—the skull.*

Snatching the bone into his mouth, he sprang up. The tags on his collar jangled as he trotted over and dropped the bone in my lap. "Thanks."

Standing, I let the human bone fall to the grass. I didn't want to touch it. And that wasn't just because, well, it was once a person. It would be evidence, and I didn't want to mess with that. As promised, I scratched behind his soft furry ears.

Detective Jacobson crept toward the bone at my feet. He pulled a glove from a pocket, ready to pick it up. "He's not going to, uh, bite me, is he?"

Hooking my fingers under the dog's collar, I led him a couple feet away. A brass plate attached to the collar was engraved with "Stanley". "His name is Stanley, and he's fine. He's not the one with a gun." I tipped my head. "I'm sorry. Look, he'll show us where the rest of the bones are when you're ready. And by the way, it is human."

"*Stanley* will?" His pinched expression hardened. "Do I need to ask how you know it is in fact human and why you know where to find more, Dr. Collins?" Frowning, Detective Jacobson waved the other two over.

"*I* don't. Stanley does."

"You expect me to believe … what? That Stanley *told* you all this?"

"Hold on." I scowled at him. Dimples or not, I wasn't going to let him mock me or Stanley. "You called for my help. Remember? I didn't come here on my own. And, yes, in a way he did."

"Right." Even when he sneered, his dimples showed.

"It's not *that* weird. Lots of people can do this. I took a class a few years ago on animal communication—learned how to listen and respond to them." I shook my head, dismissing his skepticism. "It's all about images and being open and receptive, and believing what comes through." Looking up into his intense green eyes, I bit at my lower lip. "I don't know how else to explain it."

Still glaring at me, he nodded. "Okay. For now. Where? How far?"

"Just a minute." Making that connection with Stanley again, I pictured fields and fences.

Stanley twisted to the left, and the images came. *Three fields about this size, fences, jump a ditch, one more field and fence. Another ditch. Bones.*

I sighed out a long breath. "Maybe half a mile." I pointed. "That direction."

Detective Jacobson pressed a button on the side of a walkie he'd taken from another pocket. "Brent, bring me an evidence bag and contact the CSU. Let them know this isn't the primary crime scene. We'll give them an update when we have the location.

Brent's voice came back, static scraping at his words. "Copy. Since I didn't hear a shot, I take it the doc was successful?"

Glancing at me sideways, Detective Jacobson pushed the button again. "Affirmative." He tucked the walkie away again.

Hands on hips, I frowned at him.

At my side, Stanley barked out one short accusing "Woof."

Chapter 2

STANLEY BOUNDED AHEAD THROUGH THE field, turning every so often, wagging his tail and barking, urging us to hurry. At a low spot in the ground beneath the fence, Stanley slipped under the woven wire and stood still, nose up, sniffing the air.

"How are we supposed to get over the fence?" Jacobson wiped sweat from his forehead and surveyed the length of the barrier. "Is there a gate?"

The female deputy chuckled. "Come on, Ben. I'll show you how to get over."

"How about a gate? Better yet, a paved road. I'd settle for a dirt road or even a path."

"City boy," she mumbled, smiling at him.

Standing on a grassy mound next to a drooping section of barbed wire, I pushed the sagging strands down, threw one leg over, and hopped, landing unscathed on the other side.

"Come here, Ben." The deputy tried to hide her grin. She held the loose lines close to the woven wire part of the fence.

"No. No. I can do this by myself." He glanced at me and the patrolman

standing next to me on the *other* side of the fence. "If she can do it—
you're, what, five-four?"

"Yeah, and you're six-one? So?" I couldn't control my spreading smile.

He strode to the fence, close to the spot I'd climbed over. Fingers grasp-
ing the barbed wire, he jerked back. "Ouch." He examined his hand, shook
it, and, looking down, grabbed the fence again. Swinging one leg over, he
straddled the wires.

I noticed that his shiny black loafers weren't so clean anymore. And
he'd just settled one shoe in a fresh cow pie hidden in the tall grass at the
edge of the fence.

"Great." He held up the foot covered in a sticky green goo and started
to wobble. His balance on the clod of grassy dirt failing, he set his foot
again, careful to avoid the landmine. In a quick jump-hobble-hop, his pant
cuff caught on a barb. He jerked, and the sound of ripping cloth followed.
Touching down two feet from the fence, he examined the small tear and
then wiped his mucky shoe on a clump of grass.

"Are you okay?" I tried to keep the chuckle out of my voice, but I
failed.

Brushing his hands, he smirked. "I'm fine. Thank you."

We managed the next three fences and two ditches without any further
mishaps.

His movements wary, Stanley approached the edge of the ditch and
whined, pawing at the loose soil.

I took a step closer, standing behind Jacobson and the female deputy.
Peering between them, I stared down into slow-moving water. The empty
eye sockets of a human skull stared back at me. Retreating, I gasped. "Okay.
If you don't need me, I'll take Stanley home now."

"Wait. I'm still not completely buying Stanley told you— But how—"
His brilliant green eyes narrowed and he shook his head, staring at me.
"You did *follow* the dog."

I stuffed my hands in my pockets. "No, I followed you, and *you* followed Stanley. So how do you explain that?"

Detective Jacobson continued to stare at me, his glare piercing. He
glanced at Stanley, reached down, and scratched behind the dog's ears.

"You did get him to give up the bone, too. I saw that." He straightened and looked around at cross-fenced pastures.

The female deputy tipped her head. "Are you like a dog whisperer or something?"

"Not exactly. I took a class on animal communication and was good at it." I nodded. "Am good at it. And, being a vet, it comes in handy. And it's not just dogs, but all animals." Heat rushed up my neck and into my cheeks.

"I've heard about that. There was a woman in Portland … helped out sometimes at the zoo. Saw it in the paper." She looked at me and nodded. "So, it really works."

I shrugged. "Most of the time. It's just like people, though—not everyone wants to talk."

She keyed the mic secured on the epaulet of her khaki uniform shirt. "Brent, I'm sending you GPS coordinates. We're behind a barn about a half mile west of your position. We'll need crime-scene tape, and let the CSU know."

Between blasts of static, Brent answered, "Copy. On my way."

Jacobson stepped back, motioning me to follow. "Too bad Stanley can't tell us who this is, how they got here, and why." His eyebrows rose, and he watched me.

The heat of his stare made me uneasy. I shifted from one foot to the other, my gaze drifting to Stanley. "It might be possible to find out, if he knows."

"Can you ask him?" He smiled.

"Are you making fun of what I do, or do you believe me now?"

"'Believe' might be a stretch. Let's just say I don't think you had anything to do with this body or how it got here."

A line of official vehicles turned into the long driveway at the front of the property. An older man, bald head reflecting the bright sunlight, walked from the back of the barn and toward the impromptu meeting taking place in the pasture.

Probably his pasture.

"Looks like I'm on." Jacobson took a step, stopped, and pivoted to face

me. "Thanks for your help, Doctor Collins." He smiled, green eyes sparkling. "And thank Stanley for me, too." Head tipped, he pointed at my shirt.
"You have a little something there. Barbeque sauce?"

    "Oooo. A man who knows his sauce." I fanned my face with my hand
and chuckled.

Chapter 3

THE IMPERIAL MARCH BLARED FROM my phone, startling a woman standing at the front desk who was obviously not a Star Wars fan. The Chihuahua in her arms began to shake. "Sorry." I grimaced, tossed the chart I was reading to the counter, and pulled the phone out of my pocket. "Gracie, hi."

My best friend screeched in my ear, loud enough that I didn't need to hold the phone close or have it on speaker. "Why didn't you tell me you found a dead body?"

The woman with the skittish little dog took a step back, her eyes wide. "I'll just be … sitting … over … here." Cradling him, she dashed away, craning her neck to glare back at me.

"Hold on," I whispered at a still-questioning Gracie. Hurrying to the nearest empty exam room, chased by Eric's laughter, I closed the door behind me. "How did you find out?"

"It's all over the news."

"How did they find out?"

"I don't know. A PR rep was giving the reporters a statement."

"Which channel?"

"All of them. They said the body was found outside Eagle Point over the weekend—and that along with a team of officers, a local veterinarian, Dr. K. Collins, aided in the investigation."

My phone beeped, alerting me to another call—my mother. "I'll have to call you back."

"Your mom?"

"Yup."

"Good luck. And you better call me. ASAP."

"I will. Tonight." I switched lines. "Hello, Mom."

Sticking his head into the room, Eric said, "You have a call on line two. It's your police friends."

"Kallie, dear, what's this about you finding a body?"

I gave Eric a thumbs up, and he disappeared through the closing door. "Mom, I can't talk right now. I'll call you tonight, okay?"

"Your father is very concerned. He's worried about you. You need to call me back."

"I promise. And don't worry. I'll talk to you later." I tapped *end call* and picked up the phone in the exam room, punching the blinking button. "Hello. Dr. Collins speaking."

"Dr. Collins, this is Detective Jacobson. I'm calling to give you a heads up. We've released information on the body found outside Eagle Point Saturday and your name—"

"Too late."

"What?"

"It's already on the TV news."

"Umm, it's only four."

"Yeah, well, one station does an early newscast at that time. They're probably running it as breaking news, and the other stations, not to be out-done, are interrupting their regular programs with the headline."

"I didn't know that. Sorry. But in my defense, I just found out myself." He took in a deep breath and let it out in a long sigh. "Any problems yet?"

"Well, my mom called, demanding to know why I was involved."

"Uh oh. Again, sorry."

"That's okay. Have you found out who it is?" I rubbed my forehead. "Never mind. I know you can't say."

"Not yet. I'll let you know when I can. By the way, how's Stanley?"

"Ah, Stanley." I chuckled. "He's good. His family was glad to see him. Seems he keeps digging out of the yard. They're going to work on that."

"Well, thanks again, Doc."

"You're welcome, Detective."

"Call me Ben."

"Okay, Ben. I'm Kallie."

"Kallie, thanks. I'll call you. I mean, to let you know what's happening in the case. You know … when I can."

"Sure. Thanks, Ben. Bye." I hung up, my stomach doing those crazy somersaults again, but not the bad kind this time. Chuckling, I mumbled to the empty room, "Well, he is cute. And kinda nerdy. I like that in a man."

After a long conversation with my parents, and assuring them repeatedly I was never in any danger, I arranged to meet Gracie and Sam, my two best buds since college, at Rockin' Rodeo. It's a family-friendly bar and grill that, oh happy coincidence, has line dancing on Tuesday and Thursday evenings.

We ordered burgers, sweet-potato fries, and iced tea. After the server left, they both turned on me, demanding every detail.

I started from the beginning, including my mom's attempt to set me up with Eddie.

Our meals came.

They ate.

I talked, finishing with the phone call from Ben.

Gracie dipped a fry in a small bowl of honey-mustard sauce. She held it halfway to her lips and stared at me, her hazel eyes bright with curiosity. "So are you going to see him again?"

Frowning, I shrugged. "What? Stanley? I doubt it."

Sam almost spit out a mouthful of iced tea. She tossed long blond hair over one shoulder, grabbed a napkin, and wiped her lips. "Ben. Sheesh, girl."

"Oh. I don't know. Probably not. I mean, I'd like to know what they find out, but I guess all that will be on the news." I hadn't said anything about how cute I thought Ben was—well, nothing about his dimples and those intense green eyes anyway. *Okay. Stop already. Am I that obvious?*

Sam and Gracie looked at each other and shook their heads.

"What?" I muttered around a mouthful of bacon cheeseburger. My phone vibrated against the table. Chewing and licking ketchup from my fingers, I picked it up. A number I didn't recognize showed at the top of the screen. I swallowed and swiped. "Hello?"

"Hey, it's Ben. Sorry to bother you."

"No, Ben. Hi. This is fine. What's up?"

Gracie mouthed, "Put him on speaker." Brown chin-length hair was swinging with her enthusiastic nodding.

Her brown eyes wide, Sam clapped her hands.

I shook my head, placing a finger over my lips to quiet them.

"I need you. I mean, the department needs your assistance again. We've found the deceased's home and family. I know you're not on duty, but your boss said he'll authorize your overtime and travel. Will you help? I'll give you the location."

"Sure. Just a minute." I dug through my bag for a pen and a piece of paper. "Go ahead. What's the address?"

"It's out in the hills beyond Ashland. The address is a little confusing. Can I text you GPS coordinates?"

"Yes, I can do that." My phone buzzed and a line of numbers showed up. "Got it."

"Good. See you in an hour?"

"On my way." I lowered the phone and then pulled it back up. "Wait. Ben?"

"I'm here."

"What is it? I mean, is everything okay?"

"I need your animal-communication skills again. You see, there's this cat ..."

Chapter 4

THE WARM FALL SUNSHINE OF the day gave way to a chilly evening. The farther I got from the city, the brighter the stars shone, winking into view against the velvety backdrop of a cold night sky. I lost service as I entered the hills and picked it back up about fifteen miles later. The road narrowed to one lane. Tall trees leaned out over switchback curves. Headlights pierced the dark, illuminating a short forward swath of pavement and dirt shoulder. Dark encompassed me from both sides.

Kinsey Millhone, that small-town gumshoe from the alphabet mysteries books by Sue Grafton, whispered from my speakers as she hid in a dumpster from the killer stalking her.

"Perfect." I sighed and glanced right and then left out the side windows. Shadows grew and jumped as I slowed for another hairpin turn. "Kinsey will be okay. I'm only halfway through the alphabet. She's fine. I am, too." So I continued to listen and drive up the dark, winding, tree-covered road to nowhere. "Not nowhere—to the possible scene of a murder."

A blink of red flickered ahead between low limbs. Around another sharp curve, more lights appeared, red and blue, flashing in the dark like a beacon of safety.

I let out a long breath I hadn't realized I'd held. "Sheesh, Kallie. Get a grip." Pulling to the side of an Oregon State cruiser, I stopped. An officer in uniform stood guard at the end of a long uphill drive, keeping out the curious or any news reporters that might venture that far.

But I didn't see Ben. I peered up the long dark driveway. "Probably at the house," I muttered. "At least I hope there's a house, somewhere."

A hand appeared in my peripheral vision and tapped on my window. Jumping, I stifled a scream that came out in a high-pitched squeal. Clutching at my chest, I rolled down the glass.

Ben hid a smile. "I didn't mean to scare you." He controlled the grin and opened the door.

"It's okay. It was just a creepy drive." I climbed out of my truck, slipped into a hooded sweatshirt I'd pulled from behind the seat, and looked around. "Wherever this is."

"Yeah. I should've warned you. Pretty remote area."

"No. You told me—the confusing address. I get it." I squinted into the dark past the cruiser, its light bars blinking with a rapid ticking. Beams in the distance lit glimpses of low brush but nothing else. "Is there a house? Where is this cat? Is she okay?"

"I'll walk you up, but I need you to stay outside until we're finished talking to the family." Ben motioned for me to follow him.

"Sure. Of course. I can't imagine having to break the news that some-one has died."

Ben stopped and looked at me. "It's never easy. We don't have DNA confirmation yet, or dental records—just a wallet with Mr. Whedon's iden-tification inside." He gestured up the hill. "But I think they expected this outcome. They reported him missing over a year ago."

We continued up a steep drive. Glancing at him, I noticed Ben wasn't wearing a suit. Instead, he wore a brown leather jacket over a light-colored button shirt, blue jeans, and boots. Maybe the last outing had him rethink-ing his wardrobe choices. Remembering his shoe landing in the cow pie, I bit at my lip to stop from smiling.

"What?"

"Nothing." Not able to control my reaction, I smiled and gestured. "Nice look."

"Oh, yeah." He chuckled. "Well, after last time, I figured suits and loafers may not be the best idea here."

"You're new in the area?"

"Yes. I was working in Portland until … until I started here almost a month ago." He grinned. "I rarely needed to traverse mucky fields, scale fences, or jump muddy ditches there."

"Well, it's a nice look." Heat flooded my cheeks. "And much more practical."

"Thanks."

I didn't see the house until we passed the barn. Four more vehicles, two unmarked, were parked just below a large front deck. I followed Ben up the steps.

"Wait here." Ben pointed toward a grouping of chairs around an empty metal fire pit. "Captain Granger, my boss, doesn't want to upset the family with, um, what you do. He's not quite sure he believes, but he can't explain how you were able to help us earlier. He's willing to try this. His main concern is not turning this into a media free-for-all with reports of the sheriff's department using psychics and ghost whisperers."

"But I'm not either of those."

"I know and he knows. I think." He held up his hands. "We just want to keep this quiet."

"Okay. I prefer my name and what I do stays out of the news, too." A frown tightened my forehead. "How did you find out about the cat?"

A silhouette appeared at the open front door.

"I'll explain later." Ben took my arm, leading me to the closest chair. "I'll be right back."

Sitting, I listened to muted voices coming from inside and caught snippets of conversations. Interior illumination painted off-kilter squares and rectangles of muted amber light on the decking outside the windows and the open door. Above me, bright stars covered the dark night sky peeking between tall stands of pines and broad oaks. A cool breeze hurried dry yellow leaves skittering across redwood planks.

A slight rhythmic clicking sounded on the deck. At my left, a dog emerged from the shadows, glanced in my direction, and angled her path straight toward me. She trotted over and sat down at my feet, staring up at me with big brown eyes.

"Hello." I held my hand an inch or so from her long nose. "Corgi-terrier mix. Nice."

A quick lick followed a perfunctory sniff.

"Yeah. Lots going on. I guess someone you know died." Smoothing the soft fur on her head, I moved my fingers back to scratch behind warm, small pricked ears. "It'll be okay."

Sometimes the images come without my asking.

A dark close space. Musty scent of damp soil. The dirt on her belly cool. Napping until yelling from above wakes her. Another noise. Sharp. Loud. Scrambling back, she stares out through a small rectangle of light.

Her fear enveloped me like a thick fog.

More noise. More yelling. Close. Something small darts through the rectangle, blocking out the light for a second—the cat. It settles beside her, watching. They stay quiet.

Legs block the light again. Two men. Dragging another man. Worn brown boots and faded jeans. Long dark hair and an unkempt beard. Dust drifting in the dry air. Cat turns and disappears into the dark background. They drag the man through the backyard and then a gate. Into the brush, the woods. Different noise. Boom. Boom. Boom. Running legs. Car noise. Gone.

Quiet. Dark. Stay. Safe.

No cat. Alone.

Sun down. Sun up. Crawling out from the safe dark into cool morning sunshine. House quiet. Bowls. Cool water. Good food.

Alone.

My heart pounded in my chest. Whatever had happened, happened there, in the house, and this dog was present. Well, she was under the house but able to see enough to give me a clear picture. I moved to a seat for two and invited the dog to sit with me. She hurried over and jumped up, snuggling in next to me. Taking several deep breaths, I petted her. Long slow strokes calmed me more than her. I brought a picture to my mind. *Where? An image of the man with the brown hair and beard, being dragged into the brush behind the house. Little miss corgi following the path they took.*

Images flooded my mind.

Panting. Sun hot. Buzzing bees. Snap at the flies. A narrow path under the brush. Not far. Sniffing. Squirrels. Rabbits. No brush. No man. Dirt. Sticky like mud. Dark. Dig. Nothing. Sniff. Sneeze.

"Okay, thanks." I patted her head, adding another image of my own. *Her leading me to the digging place.*

Jumping down, she landed on the deck, wiggled, and spun, her stubby tail wagging furiously.

Standing, I looked toward the door. Quiet conversations trickled out into the cool night air. *Should I tell Ben? Well, yes, but he's busy and besides, it won't hurt to check it out first. It may be nothing.* I pulled my phone from my pocket and opened the flashlight app. "I'll be careful. I won't disturb anything." I followed her around the side of the house, onto the long back deck, and down the stairs into the yard. She led me across thick damp grass, where she slipped through a small hole in the six-foot chain-link fence and disappeared in tall yellow weeds and dense brush.

"Wait," I called in a hoarse whisper.

The weeds shook and she reappeared, staring up at me.

My gaze traveled the fence line, searching for … "There it is." I stepped to the gate, lifted the latch, and tugged, but it only opened a few inches before getting stuck on clumped, uneven ground.

She yapped, her stumpy tail wagging in excitement.

"Shhh." I put a finger to my lips. "Quiet, little missy."

Settling down, she sat. Her tail still wagged, jiggling her furry body up to her ears.

"I'm right behind you. Just don't go too far ahead." I squeezed through the barely open gate, keeping the light focused on my little guide. She navigated her way beneath the dense weeds and bushes, nose to the ground.

My path was not so straightforward. Stepping over the lowest patches of dry brush and dragging my feet through the taller bunches, I knew my legs would be a scratched-up, itchy mess by the end of this, despite my jeans.

The small clearing appeared in a ring of pines and small cedars. She ambled into the center and teased at the thin surface of dry needles with one paw.

Moving inside the brush-free area, I shined my light at the ground. Nothing—at least not that I could see. Thin light bathed the area in front of me, as I crept toward the center.

Corgi girl dug with more enthusiasm, both paws tearing at the loose soil, dirt flying behind her. She'd stop, stick her nose into her work, snort, chuff, and continue. Her snorting turned to a soft growl as she tugged at something she'd unearthed.

"Whoa, stop. Come here." I clapped my hands to get her attention. Backing up, I knelt at the edge of the circle, my meager light directed toward the bundled cloth she'd unearthed. "Come here. Come on. Good girl."

She let go of her prize and tottered over, snuffling and sneezing, her nose covered in dirt.

"Good girl," I repeated and wiped her face, cleaning dust from around her eyes and off her cool, moist nose. "What did you find?"

Turning, she sat beside me, and we both stared at the wad of light-colored cloth peeking from the soil. My pulse jumped to a faster tempo. *I hope that's not another body.*

A low growl started deep in her chest. She turned her head to watch behind us.

"What is it?" I listened. Shining my light behind, around, and to the far side of the circle, I stopped on two yellow eyes glaring at me from under low limbs.

Her growling rose, and she let out a high-pitched rapid-fire burst of barks.

Brush rustled behind me.

We both stood up and spun at the same time. Between her under my feet and the loose soil, I dropped my phone, the light blinking out, and I almost fell.

Except Ben caught me.

Chapter 5

"WHAT ARE YOU DOING OUT here?" Ben set me back on my feet and glanced at the dog circling his legs, her tail wagging. "And who is this?" Not waiting for an answer, he let go of my arms. He pulled a flashlight from his pocket and shined the narrow beam around the cleared area, stopping on the twisted wad of cloth. "What is that? How ..." Hunching down, he squinted, angling the beam. He picked up my phone and handed it to me.

From behind us a male voice called, "Ben, you okay? Did you find her?"

"Yes. We're here," he shouted. "About thirty feet in. Send in a crew with an evidence kit." Standing, he took my arm and turned me toward the house. "Let's get you and your little friend out of here."

Before we'd gone ten feet, a uniformed officer pushed through the brush. "What is it?"

"Maybe nothing. Better check it out, though. Looks like a piece of clothing buried in a clearing." He gestured over his shoulder. "Keep straight. Another twenty feet."

Flashlights bobbed ahead as more officers approached.

Back on the deck, my little friend darted away and into the open front door.

A woman knelt and scratched the dog's neck. "Ariel. Are you being a good girl?"

Glancing at me, Ben frowned. His face smoothed, and he asked, "Mrs. Whedon, the woods beyond the backyard ... Is that part of your property?"

Ariel in her arms, Mrs. Whedon straightened. "That's public land, I think." She tipped her head. "Why do you ask?"

"Just curious."

During their conversation, I took a moment to look around. It was a spacious two-story log home, decorated by someone with a taste for refined items and the budget to go with it. Across from the entry, a family portrait hung on the wall—a man, a woman, and two teenage children, a boy and a girl. The woman stood before me holding a wiggling Ariel. She looked pretty much the same, right down to her short, perfectly styled, light-brown hair.

But the man ... He had pale blond hair and was clean shaven. Unless he'd dyed his hair almost black, and the same with a six-month beard growth, this wasn't who was dragged into the woods. It didn't mean the man in the picture wasn't dead. It just meant he wasn't whom the dog, and the cat, saw that day. *So when did that happen, and who was it?*

Ben introduced me. "Mrs. Whedon, this is Dr. Collins. She consults sometimes on cases."

"Hello, Mrs. Whedon. I'm so sorry for your loss." Possibilities crashed against each other inside my mind. *Could her husband be alive? Could he be the murderer? Is there more than one? Murderers and bodies?*

"Thank you, Dr. Collins. And thanks for helping."

"Detective Jacobson, why don't you take Dr. Collins into the kitchen and brief her." This had to be Captain Granger, Ben's boss. He stared at me with steely eyes, his forehead bunching under short cropped gray hair.

"Yes, Captain." Ben nodded to me. "This way, Dr. Collins."

As soon as we reached the quiet of the kitchen, Ben opened his mouth to talk, but I cut him off. "Can you find out when the picture in the foyer was taken?"

"Yes. I mean, I already know." Ben frowned. "Why?"

"How long before Mr. Whedon disappeared did they have it made?"

Ben's frown deepened and he leaned forward. "About a month. It was the picture they used for Mr. Whedon's missing case file."

Biting my lip, I turned toward the kitchen window overlooking the backyard and forest beyond.

"Kallie, what is it?"

"Ariel showed me something." I spun. "An unconscious man with dark, almost black hair and a full beard was being dragged across the lawn, past the fence, and into the woods by two other men."

"But Mr. Whedon was blond, no beard … and his body, or one with his ID, was found miles from here."

"Exactly."

"That would mean …" Ben's attention snapped to the kitchen window. "Who did the dog see, and when? Before or after Mr. Whedon's disappearance?" His focus shifted to me. "Can you find out?"

"Maybe. I'd need some time with Ariel—a lot of time. If we're talking over a year ago, I can't pin it down to an exact day. Maybe the season."

"How can you be sure the dog saw anything?" Ben rubbed at his forehead. "I mean, maybe she's confused about what she saw, or wrong, or—"

"Dogs don't lie. They can't. It's against an animal's nature to purposefully deceive. And why would they? For what reason? Only humans—"

"Okay. I get it. But—"

"I know what I saw." I leaned toward Ben, my jaw set. "The man in the picture was not the same one who was dragged through the yard."

Captain Granger walked in. "What's going on out back?"

The kitchen door flew open. An officer rushed in holding a plastic evidence bag with the dirty cloth from the clearing inside. "Captain," he panted. "We found this buried in the woods, just behind the house. Can't be sure, but it looks like old dried blood on a man's shirt." He handed Granger the bag. "We're setting up a perimeter and calling in the CSU, in case there's more."

Glancing at me and then Ben, Granger sighed. "You want to tell me what's going on, Ben?"

"It was me, sir." I stepped forward. "I was sitting outside when the Whedons' dog, Ariel, came over to me." Taking in a deep breath, I continued. "She showed me, from her point of view under the house, or the deck, a man with long brown hair, almost black, and a scraggly beard being dragged by two men—I couldn't see their faces—beyond the fence."

"A man with long dark hair and a scruffy beard." He took in a slow, deep breath and crossed his arms. His attention snapped back to Ben. "And this is how you found"—he held the bag out—"this?"

"Yes, Captain."

Handing it back to the officer, Granger turned on me. "How do I explain this to Mrs. Whedon? Or the courts, if it comes to that?"

"Tell them the truth." I bit my lip, frowning at him. "I find that works best. Besides, I didn't seek you out. I'm not asking for money. I'm certainly not looking for publicity. In fact, in the future, I'd rather you keep my name out of this altogether."

"Okay." Granger nodded, his head bobbing to a slow rhythm only he heard. "O—kay." He shifted his attention to Ben. "I thought you brought her here to, uh, talk with the cat? You never mentioned a dog."

"I didn't know about the dog." Ben stuffed his hands in his pockets. "And it seems the cat isn't here."

"It's gone?"

"No." I recalled the glowing eyes on the far side of the clearing. "The cat was out back with Ariel and me."

"Sounds like you two have a cat to find." Granger gestured to the door. "I'll be with Mrs. Whedon." He shook his head and grunted. "Telling the truth."

Ben and I followed the officer, stopping at the top of the steps to the lawn.

"Well, where do we start searching?"

"For a cat?" I glanced at him, knowing an expression of skepticism crossed my face. "One doesn't usually go looking for a cat. You wait for the cat to seek you out."

"Great."

I took two steps down and sat, patting the spot next to me. "Relax. The cat showed herself once. She'll come around again—maybe."

Sighing, Ben joined me. "That's encouraging." He stared up at a swatch of night sky visible at the tops of pine, cedar, and fir trees.

"Bet you don't see stars like this in Portland."

He took in a deep breath and then chuckled. "No. And it doesn't smell quite like this either."

Inhaling the mingling scents of the trees, decaying leaves, and damp soil, I nodded. "While we're waiting, tell me why you think the cat knows something important to start with."

"Mrs. Whedon said the cat is—was—her husband's. Said it never left him. So when she returned late Sunday evening after a weekend trip with the kids to her mother's in Newport, her husband and the cat were gone. His car was still in the garage. There was no note, no phone messages—nothing. The cat showed up the following Tuesday full of burs and foxtails. By then Mrs. Whedon had contacted the police." He pulled his gaze from the sky and turned to me. "I thought ..." he shrugged. "The cat might have ... Wow. I don't even know how to phrase this. Witnessed something?"

"That works." Arms on my knees, I stared at the night sky. "If an animal chooses to share with me, I can see images and pictures—like a video. Sometimes the connection is so strong I can hear, feel, smell, and even taste what they do, or did at the time. I guess it depends how vivid the recollection is and how much time has passed for them." I frowned, biting at my lip. "That's what troubles me about Ariel's, uh, memories. I sensed everything crystal clear."

"Is that common? I mean, to get such clear ... visions?"

"Sometimes. If it's a recent event or traumatic." I tipped my head. "It could be Ariel—the kind of dog she is. She has corgi in her, and some terrier. Smart dogs. I've found border collies and poodles will practically have full conversations with me. They're so smart it's scary." I grinned. "You have to watch what you say around them."

"What about cats?"

"Cats are smart, too. But they're different than most other animals."

"As in?"

I smiled. "They do things on their schedule, not ours."

"That doesn't sound promising."

A small warm body rubbed against my back. Faint purring transferred across my skin like a vibrating motor. "We have company."

Twisting his upper body with a quick left and then right, Ben startled the cat, sending her racing to the far side of the deck.

The cat glared at Ben, her yellow eyes glowing and her back arched.

"Don't spend a lot of time around cats, do you?"

"Sorry." His movements slow and more controlled, he faced the lawn again. "Will she come back?"

"Yeah. Just give her a minute." I inhaled and let the air out slowly. "She's curious about what's going on."

A white head appeared between us, ears tipped with orange and black. A sleek body followed—white with patches matching her ears. She sat and stared out at the back woods.

"Hello, miss."

"How do you know she's a she? Did she tell you?" Ben's tone was calm, but he talked fast.

"She's a calico. Male calicos are rare."

"Calico?"

"Her coloring—the white, black, and orange."

"Oh. Really? Why?"

"The X chromosome is responsible for both orange and black fur. Female cats can display both because they have two X chromosomes. Males have just the one, so it's either black or orange for them, not both."

"Uh-oh. The Y chromosome talk again." Ben chuckled. His tone grew serious. "Do you think she'll talk to you?"

"I can try."

Ariel's toenails clicked across the deck. She pushed between Ben and the cat, forcing the cat onto my lap. The cat didn't seem to mind the new seating arrangement, her little motor running loud enough so there was no question she was purring.

"Do you know her name?" I stroked the cat's back and looked up at Ben. Ariel climbed onto Ben, settling down to curl on his lap.

"Somebody likes you." I took a moment to study his face. "That's a good sign."

"Sign?" He grinned, one eyebrow cocked. "Of what?"

"Well, dogs aren't easily fooled when it comes to a person's character. So if she trusts and likes you, that means you're a good person."

"Does that always work?"

I shrugged.

"Oh, to answer your question, the cat's name is Ella."

Chapter 6

I SETTLED IN, GETTING COMFORTABLE on the top step of the deck. Ella was in my lap, and Ben was trying not to stare at me as though I might spontaneously combust. Taking a deep breath, I intended to let it out slowly, but a chuckle erupted instead.

"I'm messing you up sitting here." Ben started to stand, holding Ariel under one arm.

"No. You're okay. Just don't stare at me." I reached up, grabbed his arm, and tugged him back down. "I can do this." Letting go, I composed myself, sat up straight, inhaled and—

"Hey, Ben." An officer hurried toward us from the lawn, a dirt-covered gun wrapped in a plastic evidence bag held in one hand.

The cat sprang from my lap and raced across the deck, disappearing into the dark beyond the property's edge.

Ben handed me Ariel and jumped up, taking one step down to the lawn to meet the deputy.

"We found this not far from the shirt. It's a Glock nine mil. Buried about a foot down. The magazine's half full. A bullet in the chamber."

Turning the bag in his hand, Ben's forehead furrowed. "Pretty dirty.

My guess is it's been there a while. Doubtful we'll find any decent prints. Have the lab check the bullets in the magazine, too. We might get lucky." He handed the gun back to the deputy and turned to look at me. "Sorry," he mouthed.

Setting Ariel on the deck, I smiled. "It's okay."

"I'll be right back." Ben sprinted up the stairs and into the kitchen, holding the door open for the deputy.

I stood and followed Ariel back to the front of the house. The door was closed. "Hmmm. Guess we'll sit out here."

After jumping onto the double seat, Ariel turned to watch me.

"Okay. I'll come sit with you." I pulled the hood of my sweatshirt over my head and sat, Ariel snuggling in beside me. The night breeze turned chilly, and I tugged the hood strings tighter. "So, Ariel. What did your Mr. Whedon do for a living? Did he have any bad or dangerous habits? Any vices or addictions?" I looked at the sprawling home with its well-kept gardens and lawn. "Why would someone want this man dead? Or what would make him leave his beautiful family?"

Ariel remained silent, her breathing slow and rhythmic.

Excited voices echoed from the backyard. Soft murmurs came from inside, behind the closed door.

"Yeah. Lots of questions. No answers." I slipped my phone from my pocket and hit the search app button. I typed in "Whedon, Southern Oregon" and waited. A news article regarding the disappearance of an Alexander J. Whedon from Ashland came up on the small screen. The picture matched the one on the wall in the entry. I read the highlights to a snoring Ariel. "Okay. He was a consulting specialist for R and A Land Development." My forehead bunched. "Hmmm. Could the A be for Alexander? No. Probably last names, not first." I read more. "Wife Julia, daughter Riley, and son Josh. Julia reported her husband missing on Monday, July ninth, twenty seventeen, after returning from a weekend trip to the coast with the children. Alexander didn't go due to a client meeting on Saturday afternoon."

Voices quieted. Crickets chirped. Frogs croaked. Their songs blended with the sigh of the breeze through the trees.

"Hardly seems like a dangerous line of work. But …" I switched the search to "R and A Land Development."

Ariel twitched in her sleep, chasing squirrels.

"R and A Land Development, LLC. Established March twenty sixteen. A professional corporation assisting land owners to achieve the most from their land economically while maintaining environmentally sound practices." I shrugged. "Sounds good. So who are R and A?" I scrolled farther and found nothing but a link to a one-page generic website, and another for an email address. "They're not exactly promoting the business." Glancing at the sleeping Ariel, I bit my lip and then looked around again. "Must be doing okay by word of mouth? I mean, this place is pretty nice—just secluded."

Gravel crunched on the road below, and headlights appeared at the bottom of the driveway.

Jerking awake, Ariel sat up and watched.

A white van rolled to a stop in front of the house. Techs in dark-blue jumpsuits carried equipment across the deck to the backyard, ignoring me.

Ariel growled low in her chest.

"It's okay. They're looking for answers about your Mr. Whedon." I scratched behind Ariel's ears, and she quieted, curling into a ball at my side.

Again, images sprang into my mind without my asking. This time, they originated from more than one source. Similar to when several people talk to you at the same time, I only got bits and pieces of the confusing visions racing at me.

A van—black, not white like the one that just drove in. Trees, limbs brushing by. Cool dark. Clear sky. Heat. Dust. Running water. Mud. Musty scents. Chirping birds. Two men. Pushing through brush and limbs to the clearing. Twigs snapping under their feet. The heat of the day cools. Shadows grow longer. Death. Flies buzzing. Run.

The switching of being tall and then short and then back to tall had my stomach churning. *Where are these coming from? Not Ariel or Ella. Something different. Something bigger. But what?*

"Kallie. Are you okay?" Ben knelt in front of me, his expression pinched. "Kallie. Say something."

"I'm … okay." I closed my eyes and drew in a deep breath. Holding up one finger, I kept my eyes shut. "Give me a minute." My stomach eased its roiling. I sensed Ben staring at me and imagined that look of worry and concern in his eyes turning to doubt and discomfort. I peeked at him through slitted lids. His green eyes wide, he watched me. No. He watched *over* me—with no judgment. I let out a breath through pursed lips.

"You scared me. I was talking to you, and I wasn't getting through." He nodded. "I thought, well, I didn't know what to think."

"Sorry. I kinda got blasted."

"Blasted?"

"Lots of images flying at me all at once. It's disorienting." I bit my lip. "Feels like I'm being sucked into a spinning kaleidoscope. It's only happened one other time."

Standing, Ben took my hand. "You're cold. Come on. I'll take you home."

"What about—"

"We can come back tomorrow. There's too much going on right now anyway."

Ariel jumped off the seat and trotted into the house through the open front door.

"You don't have to take me home. I can drive myself."

"Are you sure?" He tipped his head. "I can take you. I'll get your truck back into town."

I stood and my knees turned to jelly. Once again, Ben kept me on my feet.

"I'm taking you home. Sit down. Wait here. I'll get my car."

"No. Really. I'm okay."

"You said you got *blasted* one other time. What happened to you afterward?"

Arms crossed, I looked away from his piercing eyes. "I got a migraine. Threw up a couple times. Slept all the next day."

He rushed down the front steps and turned to me. "Stay put. I'll be right back."

☯

The beginning of a migraine throbbed across my forehead. Lights from on-coming cars hurt my eyes. A grimace felt permanently etched on my face. Chatter from the radio seemed amplified, the sound pounding in my ears and scraping at my brain.

Ben turned the volume to low.

"Thanks. That helps." At least my stomach was behaving … for the time being. I leaned my forehead against the cool glass of the passenger window.

"Do you need to go to the ER?" Ben's voice thrummed with tension. He peeked at me sideways. "What can I do?"

Squinting, I smiled at him. "Nothing the ER can do. But thanks. I just need to get home and sleep." Settling in the seat, I covered my head with the hood of my sweatshirt and closed my eyes. The car's motion and the soft drone of the engine lulled me. Next thing I knew, the lights of Medford flickered through the windshield of the car. The few minutes of sleep eased the pain, but it wouldn't fully retreat until I'd had several hours.

I sat up, my mind filled with questions.

"Feel any better?"

"A little. Did Mr. Whedon keep his appointment on the Saturday before he disappeared?"

"What?"

Pushing the hood back, I glanced at Ben. Even at night, the downtown lights made me wish I had my sunglasses. But they were in my truck along with my pack, wallet, credit cards, keys, and everything else. At least I had my phone. "How can I get in my house?"

"Your truck is right behind us."

"Oh." I considered looking and thought better, not wanting to jinx what relief I had.

"What did you ask me?" Ben slowed and turned right.

"Did Mr. Whedon make the meeting that kept him from going to the coast with his family the weekend he disappeared?"

"Why?" Ben frowned. "And how do you know about that?"

"I looked it up on my phone." I rubbed at my forehead—not just because it hurt, but because a thought formed and I wanted to coax it out. I wanted to entice the barely developed idea forward into the bright, piercing, colorful light that was assaulting my throbbing eyes. "Did he? And is he the A in R and A Land Development? Never mind. Probably not. So who is R and A? Why is their marketing and promotion so limited? How do they find new clients?"

"Slow down, Sherlock." Ben chuckled. "You know I can't talk about an open case." He turned down my street and into my driveway.

My truck pulled in beside us.

"Sorry." I unbuckled the seat belt.

Ben got out and took my keys from the officer who was standing in front of my truck.

Opening the car door, I clambered out, hanging on to the window frame for support. My head spun. The pain behind my eyes increased. My house was just in front of me—a few steps away. And inside was my bed, blessed quiet, and the cool dark.

Ben took my arm until I was moving under my own power. "Let's get you inside." He used the key, holding my pack with his other hand.

I'd left a light on in the kitchen, illuminating the entry and hall. "Thanks. I'm good now."

"You sure?" Ben's expression morphed from skepticism to concern. He tossed my pack on the kitchen counter.

"Yeah. Just going to put some peppermint oil on my head and go to bed."

"Peppermint oil?"

"Hold that thought for another time." I rubbed my temples. There were no thoughts swirling there anymore—just the headache.

"Will do. Got your phone?"

Squinting, I held it up for him to see.

"Call me if you need anything."

I heard in his voice that he meant it. "Thanks, Ben." I straightened, trying to appear composed. "As your consultant, wouldn't I be authorized to know about this case? A little anyway?" Frowning, I looked at him. "Do you have pictures of either R or A or both?

"Go to bed. We'll talk in the morning." He stepped outside, smiling at me before he closed the door.

Chapter 7

I'D DROPPED INTO BED THE previous night after pulling the covers back and only taking off my sweatshirt and shoes. It wasn't the most comfortable, but I slept and didn't wake until morning. Intermittent shafts of sunlight slipped through the gap in my bedroom curtains. Peeking with one eye, I tested the effect of the light. So far so good.

After a long shower, I sat at the kitchen island sipping a hot vanilla breve. Laptop open in front of me, I searched for more on R and A, whoever they were.

I found nothing.

Well, nothing new. "So, how can I find out more about them?" I closed my laptop and jumped off the stool.

Outside the kitchen window, gray clouds rolled across the sky threatening rain.

I slipped into a florescent green hooded sweatshirt, grabbed my pack, and headed out the door, keys in hand. "Even a picture would do. They should have something at their offices, right?" I entered the address from the website into my phone's GPS and hit *go*.

Twenty minutes later, I pushed through an outer door into a

redwood-paneled foyer, and looked at the directory. "R and A, room two zero one, second floor." I climbed the stairs and stopped at the first door on the left. Hand hovering, I took in a deep breath. "Just here to ask a simple question. Nothing wrong with that." I turned the knob and entered.

An older woman sat behind a desk at the back. Three armchairs lined the right side wall, and a closed door on the left finished the room. The woman looked up from her computer, adjusted her glasses, and tucked a lock of short gray hair behind one ear. "Can I help you?"

"Hi. Yes. Could I talk to, uh, someone regarding property my family owns?" Heat filled my face and I brushed a hand over my cheek. "Warm in here, huh?" I'm a lousy liar.

"Is it?" She glanced around the room as if searching out those pesky heat waves. "Maybe you took the stairs too quickly."

"Maybe." I chuckled, sounding giddy. I put on my best serious expression and waited.

She stared at me. Frowning, she tipped her head. "What is it you want?"

"Uh, this is R and A Land Development, isn't it?"

"Well, yes, but the owners don't take meetings here. It's just me." Grinning, she rolled her eyes. "I mean, I don't. I just answer the phone, pass along messages, and take care of office duties—and not too many of those." She smiled, looking at me over her glasses. "It's an easy job. Beats sitting at home watching TV and gossiping with all the ladies at the park." Winking, she flapped a hand in the air and chuckled. "That Ernestine Wilson isn't happy unless she's spreading dirt on someone." She composed herself. "I'm sorry for going on. Don't get much company here. But a pretty young lady like you isn't interested in the ramblings of an old woman."

"No. That's okay. Really." I meant it. She seemed nice. Maybe she wasn't a genius, but she was kind and I'd take that any day. "So you can make me an appointment to meet with, uh, the owner or owners?"

Her pleasant smile morphed to a frown. "You know, I'm not sure. Well, not anymore."

"You're not sure you can schedule an appointment?" I'm sure my confusion showed in my expression.

"Oh. No. I mean, yes. I can take your number, and someone will get back with you." She blushed. "As for the owners …" She shook her head. "That nice man Mr. Whedon doesn't come in anymore." She lowered her voice. "He disappeared about a year ago. And I haven't seen Mr. Smith for several months now." Her eyes closed and she nodded. Lids popping open, she continued, "No, it's been about a year, same as Mr. Whedon. I just see Mr. Johnson now, and not very often." Sitting up straight and picking up a pen, she said, "If you'll leave your name and a contact number, I'll pass it along to him."

"Great." I shuffled inside my pack for a business card. "I take it the R and A in the company name doesn't stand for the owners' last names."

"Oh. No. I think it's initials of two of their children, or maybe their wives." Her forehead creased. "I shouldn't say. I'm not really sure."

I handed her my card. "All my contact information is there."

Reading it, she smiled. "A veterinarian. Good for you, dear."

Tell that to my mom. "Thank you."

I turned toward the door but then spun back. "Would you have any pamphlets or flyers? My dad's kinda funny about these things. He likes to know about who he's doing business with."

"I understand, but, no, we don't." She smiled as if her answer was enough.

"No card either?"

Staring at me, she said nothing.

"How about anything with a picture of Mr. Smith or Mr. Johnson? A newspaper clipping? Maybe when they started the business? Like I said, my dad likes to know who he's meeting with."

She tapped a finger on her lips. "Let me think." Throwing her hands in the air, she jumped a bit in her seat. "I have a picture with both." She opened a side drawer, pulled out a glossy four-by-five photo, and handed it to me. "You can keep that, to show your dad. I have more."

"Thanks." I took the picture and looked at two smiling men and their beaming new office manager. My heart almost lurched from my chest, my mouth dry. Leaning over the desk, I pointed to a man with tousled dark hair and a neat beard—the man Ariel had showed me being dragged through the backyard. I swallowed, trying to get my mouth working. "Is this Mr.

Smith?" Pointing to the other man—older, slightly overweight, and balding—I asked, "And is this Mr. Johnson?" My tongue stuck to the roof of my mouth. "My dad will want to know."

"Oh, no, dear. You have them mixed up." She pointed to the bearded man first and then the balding one. "That's Mr. Johnson and that's Mr. Smith."

"One more question. When was this photo taken?"

"The day I started—April, two thousand seventeen. About a year and a half ago."

"Thank you. You've been very helpful."

"I'll give Mr. Johnson your number."

My voice rose in pitch. "What?"

She waved my business card in the air. "Your contact information? For your property?"

"Oh, yes." I nodded my head, grinning like an idiot. "Thank you."

As I raced down the steps, my phone vibrated and the ringtone echoed through the silent staircase. I fumbled with the buttons and finally got the blaring music to stop. "Hello? Mom? Can I call you back?"

"This will just take a second, Kallie—faster if you'll agree to meet me for lunch."

"Okay. Where?"

"The country club. One o'clock. I'll see you there. And wear a dress. You aren't working or on call today." She disconnected before I could protest.

The low miserable groaning resonating against flat wooden walls came from me. "What have I done? The country club?" I looked at Mickey on my wrist smiling up at me, mocking me, the second hand ticking away with wild abandon—time slipping past. I had a couple hours, and, dress or not, I was headed to lunch at the country club with Mom.

But first I needed to talk to Ben.

In the quiet of my truck, I called him. It went directly to voice mail and I left a message to call me. With no further excuse, I headed home to find something *precious* to wear to lunch.

◠◡

Standing in front of the closet, I stared at the row of clothes on hangers, shoes and boots lining the floor, and tidy boxes on a top shelf. It wasn't that I didn't have anything to wear. Mom handled keeping my closet full … of her choices. Determined, I nodded. "You can do this. It'll keep her happy for at least a week." I selected a knee-length dark-green dress with long fitted sleeves. After scanning the floor, I grabbed a pair of high-heeled brown suede ankle boots. I ran a curling iron through my hair and brushed on a little mascara. "Good enough."

I tried not to turn an ankle walking outside. The squeal of the driver's door reminded me it was probably time for a new truck. But … *No reason to replace what still runs.*

I reached the key toward the ignition but then paused. If I left right then, I'd be too early. I tried Ben's number again. Voicemail. I glanced at the dash clock—a little past noon. Biting at my lower lip, a frown formed. "Didn't he say he would call me this morning? Hope everything's okay." I sat there with my thumbs tapping an irregular cadence on the steering wheel. Ideas swirled and landed on … "cupcakes." On the way to the country club, I'd pass my favorite bakery. "A reward for going to lunch and wearing a dress." Plan set, I backed out of the drive.

With one each of chocolate, vanilla, and lemon stowed safely in a taped pink bakery box on the front seat of my truck, I opened the door to the country club's restaurant. Smiling, my thrilled mom waved from a window table, and she wasn't alone.

"Kallie, you look lovely."

I stepped up to the table, glancing at two other people seated there. "Thanks, Mom."

Scooting his chair back, a young man stood and smiled at me.

"Kallie, this is Jeffrey." She gestured to the man who stood grinning at me. "And this is my good friend Olivia, Jeffrey's mother."

Good friend? I've never seen or heard of her before.

"Hi. Pleasure to meet you." I nodded to Olivia and smiled back at Jeffrey.

"I've heard nice things about you, Kallie. It's good to meet you." Jeffrey pulled a chair out for me.

I tried to sit, leaning forward at the same time, coordinating Jeffrey's efforts with my own. Somehow I managed to get close enough to the table despite his *help*. With that awkward operation out of the way, I shot a glare at Mom. "You didn't tell me we'd have company."

"It was a last-minute date, dear. Olivia walked into the salon during my appointment this morning. We started up a conversation and realized we had a lot in common. She told me her son was visiting, and here we are." She smiled and gestured around the room with a flourish.

"Yes. Here we are," I repeated. "How nice."

Setting her water glass down, Olivia looked at me. "Your mother tells us you're a doctor, a veterinarian. That must be exciting."

"Yes, it is."

Mom patted my hand. The pat turned into a warning squeeze.

Well, I couldn't blame her. She had heard me in action a time or two, so I understood her concern, especially during lunch at a restaurant at the club. I assuaged Mom's fear and kept my answer vague. "But most of the time it's fairly routine."

A waiter appeared, handing out menus and filling water glasses.

"Thank you, Patrick." I smiled, knowing him from previous visits.

"Could I start you off with something to drink?" He looked around the table.

Mom, Olivia, and Jeffrey ordered iced tea.

"Pepsi, please." I watched him walk away and then buried my nose in the menu, searching until I found what I knew was already on the menu— my regular choice, a bacon cheeseburger and sweet-potato fries. *I'm good.*

Patrick returned, set our drinks on the table, and then stood ready, pen and pad in hand.

Placing her menu down, Mom looked up. "I'll have the Caesar salad, please."

"Oh, that sounds good. Make that two, please." Olivia set her menu on Mom's.

Nodding, Jeffrey laid his menu on the others. "Make that three, please."

Patrick pivoted in my direction, pen poised. "The regular, Dr. Collins?"

Grinning, I plopped the menu on the table. "Yes. Thank you, Patrick."

Jeffrey removed his glasses and cleaned them on his white cloth napkin. He glanced over at me. "Let me see. Your regular is a hamburger. No. A cheeseburger. And onion rings?"

"Close. Bacon cheeseburger and sweet-potato fries." I frowned. "How'd you know?"

"Just a lucky guess." He cocked one eyebrow and tipped his head.

I'm sure my skepticism still showed in my expression. "Sure."

Mom beamed at him. "Jeffrey teaches computer science at SOU. Isn't that interesting?"

Okay. She had my attention. "That's great. But I thought you were visiting?"

"I just got the job. I'll be starting winter term. I'm here looking for a place to live."

"Well, good luck. It's not exactly a buyer's market right now."

"That's what I hear." He put his glasses on. "But I'm in no hurry. I may even decide to build. In the meantime, I could rent."

With his dark frames in place, I noticed his clear-blue eyes and how his light-brown hair was a little shaggy, with gold highlights.

I know women who would pay big bucks for his natural color.

Our meals came. We talked. It wasn't such a bad lunch. But I had still earned my cupcakes.

"Jeffrey, since Kallie's work takes her all over the county, she knows the area well. Maybe she could help in your search." Mom glanced at a nodding Olivia.

"Oh, that's a great idea." Olivia looked at me. "Kallie, what do you think?"

Sitting back, Jeffrey waved his hand. "No. I can't impose. She has a challenging career that keeps her busy enough." He glanced at me, his grin sheepish. "But maybe, if it didn't take too long, we could meet for coffee and I could quiz you on areas?"

"Um, sure. I could do that."

"Good." Mom grabbed the check and dug her credit card from her wallet. "It's settled, then."

Back in my truck, I checked my phone. Ben had sent a text.

Kallie. Sorry I didn't get back to you. Been in meetings. Hope you're feeling better. I'll talk to you later.

The phone vibrated in my hand, and I answered before my ringtone started. "Hey, Gracie. What's up?"

"Sam and I are meeting later for dinner. My house. I'll be home in a few minutes. She's coming about seven. Want to come?"

The thought of eating almost made me groan. "I just had a big lunch with Mom, but I'll join you for the company."

"How'd that go?"

"Actually, pretty good. I'm even wearing a dress."

Sam yelled in the background, Gracie's phone obviously on speaker. "Oh, don't change clothes. I wanna see you in a dress."

"Where are you?"

"I stopped by the hospital with some books and then into the ER to invite Sam. We're in the break room."

"Hi, Kallie," Sam called. "Wear the dress."

"Fine, I'll wear it. And I want to tell you about Jeffrey, Mom's latest attempt to set me up."

"Jeffrey? What happened to Ben?"

My phone buzzed. "Nothing. In fact, I gotta go. He's calling me right now."

A chorused "ooooooo" came from the phone before I switched calls.

"Hello, Ben."

"Well, you sound much better."

"I am. Thank you."

"I'm on a quick break. Just wanted to check in. Can I call you later this evening?"

"Yes. I have some questions about Mr. Whedon. Also, I know who Ariel saw being dragged through the backyard. It's Mr. Johnson from R and A Land Development. Thing is, he is alive, but—"

"What? Where did you find … Kallie, you need to stop looking into this. If someone doesn't appreciate your nosing around, it could be dangerous."

"Dangerous?"

A distant voice echoed through my phone, as if the speaker was down a long hallway. *"Ben, we're starting again."*

"I need to go. Don't do anything else. I'll talk to you tonight." He clicked off.

Staring at my phone, I hit the end button. "Fine. I wasn't going to anyway."

I stopped by my house before meeting my friends. After carrying the pink box with the cupcakes inside, I set them on the counter. I moved down the hall and turned into the small guest bedroom that doubled as my office to check my messages and email. Back in my room, I pulled a book off my nightstand and my leather jacket from the closet.

As I passed the kitchen on my way to the living room, I made a noble decision to take my treats and share them with my friends. Everyone needs a cupcake fix now and then. I glanced toward the counter and froze. My breath locked in my constricted chest. My pulse pounded in my ears. The once pretty pink box had a ten-inch butcher knife driven into it. A dent divided the thin cardboard top, and its sides bulged. Looking around and listening for the slightest sound, I tried to control a sudden case of the shakes.

Ben's words repeated in my mind. *Kallie, you need to stop looking into this. If someone doesn't appreciate your nosing around, it could be dangerous.*

Too late.

"Breathe. Just breathe." I took a tiny step in retreat and then another, listening for someone coming up behind me. The hair on the back of my neck stood up. My skin turned ice cold. I spun around. My head swiveled from right to left and back again, trying to see in all directions at once. I reached for my pack on the counter. Gasping for breath, my heart hammering, I ran out of the house and slammed the front door.

I managed to open my truck and climb in. Fingers trembling, I fumbled the key into the ignition and shifted into reverse. My foot slipped off the clutch. *Darn heels.* The truck lurched backward and the motor died. "Come on. Come on." I glanced at the house, imagining eyes watching me from the shadows. Heart hammering, I twisted the key. The engine took, and I backed onto the street.

Visions of intruders, knives, and ruined cupcakes swirling in my mind, I drove on automatic pilot to the closest place I'd feel safe. I misjudged the curb at Gracie's townhome and bounced into her driveway. After lurching to a stop, I turned the truck off and the engine whined into silence. I sat there catching my breath, willing my heartbeat to slow.

Gracie tapped at my window, and I screamed. Not a squeal. Not a whimper. A scream.

Matching me for pitch and intensity, Gracie threw her mail five feet in the air. "Kallie," she yelled. "What is wrong with you?"

Scrambling out, I grabbed Gracie's arm and hung on to her. "Someone was in my house and stabbed my cupcakes."

Chapter 8

AT SOME POINT WHILE TRYING to calm me down and get a straight story, Gracie dialed nine one one.

A blue-and-white SUV, siren screaming and light bar flashing, raced up the driveway minutes after my less-than-composed arrival.

Two officers hurried inside the open front door.

Sitting next to me, Gracie waved them in with one hand and patted my shoulder with the other.

A female officer nodded to her partner. "Take a look around."

"Oh. No. It wasn't here." I stood, watching as the second officer disappeared down the hall. "It was at my house. Someone broke in—"

"Dr. Collins lives on Stoneybrook," Gracie cut in. "She found, uh, things in her kitchen, um, not as she'd left them."

Maybe she was concerned I'd start rambling about stabbed cupcakes again. I took Gracie's hand, my brow furrowing. "I'm okay now. Thanks."

The officer's eyes narrowed. "Things in your kitchen?"

Her partner joined us. "It's all clear, Carter."

Officer Carter nodded at her partner.

"But this isn't where— Okay, let me explain." I told them the whole story—how I'd walked in with a perfectly fine bakery box only to find it stabbed minutes later.

"Did you leave your front door open?" Officer Carter glanced at Gracie's wide-open door. "It might have been kids in the neighborhood."

Had I? I thought for a moment. "No, though it may not have been locked."

Officer Carter's partner hooked his fingers in his belt. "I'll call in the new location." He looked at me.

"Oh. Right." I recited my address.

"Could you come back to the scene with us?" Officer Carter turned her attention to Gracie. "Maybe your friend could drive you."

Gracie and I stared at each other and nodded. We moved to the door, both grabbing our bags.

"Wait." I stopped. "What about Sam?"

"I'll let her know what happened." Gracie rummaged in her purse and pulled out a phone.

"How about you call when we get back to"—Officer Carter glanced at me—"Dr. Collins's place?"

"Oh, sure." Gracie dropped her phone back in the bag.

☙❧

Two blue-and-white police cars sat in front of my house with another in the driveway.

We stayed in Gracie's car parked on the street, waiting for the all-clear from the police.

The rain finally came, running in rivulets down the windshield and tapping on the roof.

I shivered but wasn't sure if I was cold or still spooked. Maybe both.

Gracie took the time to call Sam and update her on the situation. "She'll call before she comes to my house, to make sure we're there."

A uniformed officer came to the car. "Your front door was locked, but the French doors leading to the patio weren't. Whoever it was came through a gate in the fence back there. Glass was duct-taped and broken out on one of the panes. That's how they entered."

Not sure what to say, I stammered out a weak, "Oh."

Gracie picked up the slack. "Can we come in?"

"Sure. We have a few more questions. Maybe you could take a quick look—see if anything's missing." He opened the passenger side door.

A siren sounded in the distance, coming closer.

What now?

An unmarked sedan whipped into my drive. Ben jumped out and raced into the house.

"Ben?"

"Where?" Gracie's head pivoted, searching the area. She climbed from the car and turned to stare at me.

"He just went in the house."

"Let's go." She came around the front of her car, grabbed my hand, and towed me past the officer and toward the door. She continued to tug until we both stood just inside the small entry.

A uniformed officer photographed the bakery box on the counter, the butcher knife still protruding from the top.

My shivers returned just looking at it.

Two officers talked between the kitchen and living room, with two more checking the patio.

One appeared, walking down the hall. "It's all clear, Ben."

I hadn't noticed him coming out of the laundry room.

"Kallie." He strode over. "Are you okay?"

"Yeah. I'm fine. Just a little shook up."

"Hi." Gracie stepped up beside me. "I'm Kallie's friend. You must be the Ben we keep hearing about."

Heat burning my cheeks, I glared at her and whispered, "Stop." Turning back to Ben, I introduced her. "This is my friend, Gracie."

"Hi, Gracie. Nice to meet you." Ben turned his focus on me. "Can we talk?"

"Um, sure." I glanced at Gracie. "Be right back."

Taking my hand, *not my arm*, Ben led me to the end of the short hall. "What happened? Where did you go this morning? Who did you talk to?"

"Well, someone broke into my house and, while I was here, stabbed my cupcakes. I visited R and A Land Development, the bakery, and then lunch with my mom. As for who I've talked with, lots of people." I tried to control the frown I knew formed on my face. No luck.

He took in a deep breath. "I'm sorry. When the call came in I ... I'm glad you're okay."

"Thanks. Do you think this has something to do with Mr. Whedon's disappearance?" Frowning, I continued, "I mean, my name was in the paper and all over the news after the body was found."

His eyes narrowed. "You don't think he's dead, do you?" His focus shifted to the entry. He gestured me inside the office. Closing the door behind me, he sat me on the bed while he pulled the desk chair over. "What happened at R and A?"

"Nothing, really." I shrugged. "The office manager, the only one there, doesn't seem to know much about the business." I held up a finger. "Wait." I still had my pack over my shoulder, so I pulled out the picture. Holding it so Ben could see, I pointed to the older balding man. "This is Mr. Smith, one of the owners." I moved my finger to the bearded younger man. "This is Mr. Johnson, another owner—"

"The man Ariel showed you being dragged through the backyard at the Whedons'."

"Yes. But he's not dead. And Mr. Smith hasn't been to the office since around the same time Mr. Whedon disappeared."

"May I?" Ben took the photo and studied the two men. "Can I keep this?"

"Yes. Of course."

He slipped it in an inside pocket of his jacket. "I don't think your visit there had anything to do with this. Too quick. Probably just kids."

"Ben, I left my contact information with R and A's office manager."

"What kind?"

"A business card with my name and work phone number."

Letting out a long breath, he wiped at his forehead. "Still, this was probably unrelated. But can you stay with your parents or maybe a friend for a couple days until I check this out?"

"You think that's necessary?"

"Better to be safe."

"Sure. I can stay with Gracie."

He stood up and returned the chair. "Come on. Let's get you packed. And can you do a quick check? See if anything is missing or disturbed? Oh, and do you have a spare key? I'll make sure the doors get locked. You should contact someone right away to repair the glass. You might think about having a lock put on the back gate, too." He smiled, his green eyes sparkling. "By the way," he said as he gestured toward me, "nice look. I mean, you look nice." He waved his hand. "That is, green is a good color for you."

"Ah. The dress." Once again, heat flowed up my neck and into my cheeks. "Thanks."

Sam burst into Gracie's, throwing her bag on the counter. "Tell me everything."

Frowning, she plopped on a stool next to me and took the glass of tea Gracie offered.

"Someone got into my house through the patio—broke a glass panel out of the French doors. They think it was kids."

"But you don't?"

"I don't know. It just seems unlikely. Would kids stay in the house after I got there? Whoever it was, they were so quiet—and sneaky. You'd think they'd make noise or something.

"How do you know they were in the house with you?"

I told her the fate of the cupcakes.

"Wow." Sam shivered.

Gracie set a plate of veggies and dip in front of us and then sat next to Sam. "*I* got to meet Ben," she sang.

"Really? What's he like?" Sam grabbed a piece of celery and nibbled at the end.

"He's cute. Nice eyes. Kinda serious, though."

"Gracie, he was at a crime scene. He is a cop, you know." I picked up a baby carrot and dipped it in the honey mustard.

"So who do you think broke in?" Gracie leaned forward, staring at me around Sam.

Sam stopped chewing and watched me.

"I'm not sure how much I should tell you." I shrugged. "You already know about the body and how Stanley helped." I didn't say anything about the bloody shirt, the gun, or the men in the picture. I did mention Ariel and Ella. I added the little I'd found out about R and A and how I left my card there when I went snooping.

"Ohhhh. Probably shouldn't have done that." Gracie jumped up and checked the oven. She set out plates, silverware, and napkins.

"I get that now. Guess I'm no Nancy Drew."

Swallowing, Sam shook her head. "Now, wait a minute. Let's figure this out. What do you know about the woman in the office at R and A?"

"Not much." I frowned. "I didn't even get her name."

Oven mitt in hand, Gracie turned to face us. "She didn't introduce herself? Her name wasn't on the desk, like on a small plaque?"

"No. Neither. She was just this nice older woman—kinda nondescript." I cleared my throat. "Didn't seem overly intelligent. But the job seemed like it'd be pretty boring. I think she had a lot of time to read or play solitaire on the computer."

"Hmmm." Gracie pressed a button on the oven. "I think we should go back Monday. I'm sure the office is closed Saturday, so tomorrow's out. What's your schedule, Kallie?"

"On duty and on call for a seventy-two starting Monday. I could go Thursday."

Sam shook her head. "No. We need to do this before then. I can go with you, Gracie. Besides, it might be better if we go without Kallie. You know—new faces. You returning so soon could cause suspicion."

"I don't know, guys. I went there and a few hours later, my house gets broken into."

The timer on the oven beeped.

"I'm with Ben. I don't think it had anything to do with this. Besides, we won't use our real names." Gracie pulled a bubbling, cheesy lasagna casserole from the oven.

"Maybe we could wear disguises." Sam slid a towel over for Gracie to set the hot dish on. "I've got some different colored wigs."

They were getting way too involved in this risky adventure.

My stomach growled. Between the large lunch with Mom and all the excitement of the break-in, I didn't think I'd be hungry. But with the to-matoey, spicy aroma of the baking lasagna and buttery, garlicky French bread filling the kitchen, and seeing the finished product, I relented to pure comfort food.

We ended with chocolate ice cream, chocolate sauce, and mini choco-late chips. A carb coma was inevitable.

Set up in Gracie's guest room, I fell asleep reading one of my favorite books: *Seize the Night* by Dean Koontz. I'd read it at least a dozen times, but like comfort food, it was comfort reading.

Chapter 9

I MOVED BACK INTO MY condo Sunday night. I didn't hear from Ben over the weekend. But I did hear from Jeffrey about coffee, and we set a date for Thursday morning. I didn't feel as excited as I thought I would. My mind kept replaying reasons why Ben wouldn't contact me. *A girlfriend? A wife? Kids?*

Jumping out of my truck in the parking lot at six forty-five—that would be a.m.—I had plenty of time before shift change at seven. No other cars in the lot meant no injured or sick animals waited. *Good.*

Eric greeted me with a sleepy hello when I pushed through the front doors.

"Busy days off?" I chuckled at his mussed hair and heavy lids.

"Yeah. I helped my sister move to the coast. Nice ocean time, but I didn't get back until late last night." He yawned while holding up a large mug of steaming coffee. "The magic potion is kicking in as we speak. Just made a fresh pot."

"Perfect."

"Oh, wait. You have a message." Eric waved a pink slip over the counter.

"Thanks." I took the note without looking at it and headed to the break room. *Coffee first.* After stowing my bag in my locker, and pulling on clean scrubs over my clothes, I poured a cup, and added brown sugar and cream—real cream. Sipping the hot, sweet liquid, I headed to the small office three of us shared. At least I had my own desk. I read the note and frowned.

We need to talk. Marie.

The call had come in late Friday afternoon, but the box *not urgent* was checked.

"Who's Marie?" I turned the slip over. No phone number. No last name. Nothing. I punched a button on the desk phone. "Hey, Eric. Who is Marie? And what's her number?"

"Debbie talked to her. I guess she figured you'd know who she was and how to contact her."

"Okay, thanks." I set the note under a flap on the desk blotter. "I guess if it's important, she'll call back."

Shift change done, my morning so far consisted of a dog that needed stiches after a one-sided tussle with a raccoon, two heifers scheduled for preg checking, and a sheep with pink eye.

Eric called me on the com line. "You have a visitor."

My first thought was Marie. I headed up front, my stomach hosting a minor butterfly race.

Ben stood at the front counter. He smiled and waved.

The butterflies vanished—well, kinda. Actually, they just slipped into a happy dance. "Hey, what's up?" I didn't even try to control the grin spreading over my face.

The waiting area had three patients—a dog with a foxtail in his ear and two cats that needed stiches removed. There was nothing life threatening.

Looking at a smiling Eric, Ben asked, "Is there somewhere we could talk? It'll just take a minute."

"Sure. Follow me." I went into an exam room and called Eric. "Could you ask Brin to bring the dog with the foxtail into exam one please? Thanks, Eric."

"I can stay in here?" Ben's eyes widened. "While you, uh, do what you do?"

"It's usually a simple procedure. No blood. Nothing icky."

"Icky?" He laughed. "Is that a medical term?"

"Hang out with me a couple days, and you'll know icky."

"Hmm. Maybe I'll take you up on that offer sometime."

Brin walked the Australian shepherd in, his head tipped to one side. "This is Echo, Dr. Collins. Want me to stay and help?"

"No. I got this, Brin. Thanks. If you want to take care of suture removal, there are two cats in the waiting room." I squatted down and scratched Echo's chest.

"Right away, Dr. Collins." Turning, she smiled at Ben. "Let me know if you need me." She closed the door behind her.

Chuckling, I glanced at Ben, whose cheeks were flushed. "Well, Echo, let's see what we can do about that nasty ole foxtail." I picked him up and set him on the table. "Can you lie down for me?"

Echo did as he was asked.

"Wow," Ben exclaimed. "Did you, you know, use your communication thing with him?"

"No. He's one of those breeds that are just really smart." I took the otoscope from the wall mount, attached a green tip, and picked up a long pair of forceps with an angled end. Taking in a deep breath, I pictured Echo holding still and then me lifting his ear flap, easing the scope into the canal, and using the forceps to remove the foxtail from his ear. "It's not going to be pleasant, sweetie. But when it's all over, you will feel so much better."

Echo watched me and then laid his head down on his paws.

Snapping on the light on the scope, I lifted Echo's ear and inserted the cone.

Echo whined but didn't move.

"It's okay, baby. I see it. Now hold really still, and I'll get that nasty thing."

I reached through the tip of the cone with the forceps, gripped the fox-tail, and pulled it out.

After taking a quick look to make sure I got all of it, I let go of Echo's ear. "All done."

Echo pushed to a sitting position, his head no longer tipped to one side.

From a cabinet behind me, I took out a tube of ointment. "Now I'm just going to put some medicine in your ear. It may tickle, but it won't hurt." After a squeeze, I rubbed the base of Echo's ear.

He leaned into my hand and grinned.

"He's smiling." Ben stared at me.

"Wouldn't you?"

"That was amazing."

I picked up Echo and put him on the floor. Pressing the com, I said, "Echo's ready to go home. He needs ear ointment twice a day for a week."

"Got it all ready, Doc," Eric answered.

"What did you want to talk to me about?"

"What? Oh, yeah. I went to R and A this morning. It was empty. No office manager, no desks, no files—nothing." Ben pulled a note pad from his pocket and flipped it open about halfway. "Is this the address you went to?"

Leaning toward him, I read what he'd written and nodded. "Yes."

"There was nothing there. Are you sure that's it?"

A tap sounded at the door.

Brin poked her head in, locating Ben. "I hear Echo is ready."

"He can go, Brin. Thanks."

Brin picked up the leash and walked Echo out, but not before bestowing one last smile on Ben.

"You have an admirer."

"Yeah." Ben turned those brilliant green eyes on me. "She's not really my type."

Clearing my throat, I tapped his pad. "That's where I was—second floor, first door on the left. I can show you if you want to make sure."

"No. Sounds like the place. Thanks, Kallie. Time for me to go through the case files."

"Sorry." I frowned. "Wait a minute." I opened the door, hurried to my little office, and retrieved the note from my desk.

Ben followed, taking the slip when I handed it to him.

"I don't know a Marie." I bit at my lip. "Do you think—"

"Whoa, Sherlock. There's no reason to assume this is related in any way."

"I prefer 'Nancy,' like Nancy Drew. Or better yet, Kinsey Millhone."

He smiled. "I'll call you later. In the meantime, no more Kinsey-type adventures."

"Fine."

"Promise?"

Sighing, I nodded and held up my right hand. "I promise." I didn't make any promises for Gracie and Sam, though.

He started to walk away and then turned back. "Oh, here's your house key." After handing it to me, he pivoted and walked toward the door but then spun around again. "Um, could we have coffee? You know, to talk about the case. I feel like one, or both of us, is always in a hurry, because of outside demands and our jobs. What's your schedule like?"

"I'm pretty much tied to this place for the next seventy-two hours."

"No breaks?"

"Depends on how busy it gets."

"You stay here the whole time, even at night?" He gestured, looking at the sterile white halls and tiny exam rooms.

"There's a bedroom with a TV, table and chairs, and a shower at the end of the hall." I shrugged. "It's not that bad. If it gets too crazy, I can call for backup."

"What about eating?"

"I have food here, or I can order delivery. The techs are great. If we need something, they'll make a store run."

"Huh. Interesting." He frowned. "Okay. I'll call you tonight."

"I'll be here."

At five thirty my phone rang. I'd just settled back, feet up, thinking about dinner, and checking out Netflix. "Hello, Ben."

"Are you busy?"

"No. We can talk."

"Can I come in?"

My feet hit the floor. "You're here?"

"Is that okay? It's not against the rules?"

"No, it's fine. Where are you?"

"Walking in the door."

I hurried up front, still on the phone, until I saw Ben standing at the front desk, takeout from Best Burger in his hand. That grin filled my face again. "Hi."

"I brought dinner."

"Thank you. Come on back." The aroma wafting from the bag had my stomach growling.

Setting the bag on the table, he took out bacon cheeseburgers and sweet-potato fries, complete with honey mustard, barbeque, and ranch dipping sauce. "I didn't get drinks. Not sure what you like."

"That's okay. We have a machine here. Or water."

He glanced around, surveying the space. "So this is your home away from home?" He nodded. "You're right. It's not bad."

Looking at the small, cozy room, I saw it through Ben's eyes. Pale-blue walls. Light-gray tile floor. A twin bed pushed to one side with a dark-blue comforter and my two pillows with Star Wars pillow cases. A brown IKEA-type bookcase sat against the back wall, complete with well-worn books and a flat-screen TV on top. A round maple table and two chairs—someone's grandmother's hand-me-downs—stood under the small window. "Yeah. It's not bad." I gestured toward the door. "Do you want a soda?"

"Water's fine."

"I'll be right back." Returning with two bottles, I sat across from him. "This is great. How did you know?"

"Well, the first time we met, you had the barbeque sauce on your shirt, and I thought, hmmm." He tapped his chin with one finger while gazing at the ceiling. "Had to be bacon cheeseburgers. As for the fries," he said as he grimaced, "I guessed."

"Good job."

We both dug into the meal while it was still hot, not saying much other than small talk about the weather and other good places to eat in the valley.

Finished, I wiped my hands with a paper napkin. "Thank you so much. I needed that."

"You are very welcome." He started picking up the wrappings and tossing them in the empty bag.

"I can help." I moved to get up.

"No." He patted my shoulder. "You just relax. I think I can handle this."

He threw the bag in the garbage and returned to the table. "Kallie, can you remember anything else Ariel showed you, even if it doesn't seem important?"

Closing my eyes, I sighed. "I think it was summer." I smiled. "It smelled like it."

"How does summer smell?" His voice, calm and encouraging, came from the periphery, outside of my thoughts, from the dark boundaries around me.

"Dry. Dusty. Cedar and pine trees—their aroma in the air when it's hot outside."

"Good. Anything else?"

I took in a deep breath and let it out through pursed lips. It's difficult sometimes not to add my own interpretations, especially after so much time has passed. My eyes popped open. "Weren't we supposed to go back so I could see the cat?"

"We can do that." Ben watched me. "After last time … I mean, you getting blasted with all those visions … I just want you to be sure."

"I want to. How about Thursday?" Remembering my *date* with Jeffrey, I added, "Afternoon."

"I'll get that approved and set up a time with Mrs. Whedon."

My ringtone blared into the small space. *Uh, oh.* "Hi, Gracie. What's up?

"You'll never guess what Sam and I found." Gracie's excitement buzzed from the other end.

"That's interesting, and I'd love to hear more about your new dress, but, uh, I'm kinda busy."

"Somebody there with you?"

"Yes."

"Do you need help?"

"What? No. Nothing like that."

"Jeffrey?"

My face scrunched, and the expression leaked into my voice. "Noooo."

"Ben?"

"Yes." That silly grin came back again.

"Okay. Call me later." She disconnected.

"Gracie." I smiled at Ben as if her name explained everything—or nothing.

Ben stood. "I should let you go. Oh, there's a Star Wars marathon on SYFY tonight." He grinned and walked out the door.

I gave Ben fifteen minutes and then called Gracie back. "Okay. He's gone. What did you guys find?"

Sam yelled, "Hello."

"Hi, Sam. What did you do?"

"We went to the address you gave us." She sucked in a deep breath. "You are not going to believe this—"

"There was nothing there. All gone."

"There was— How do you know?"

"Ben told me. He went this morning."

"Oh. But I bet he doesn't know what else we found out."

I dropped onto the bed and pulled my pillows on my lap. "What?" With the office no longer there, I considered what my two good-hearted friends—one an ER nurse and the other a high school math teacher—could possibly have uncovered.

"I have a cousin that works for planning. He told me they have some questionable business practices when it comes to—how did he put it—land acquisition."

She had my attention. "Like what?"

"Like—"

The alarm sounded and a voice called over the com. "Kallie, we've got an emergency."

"Sorry. I gotta go. Talk to you later."

Chapter 10

Later ended up being a lot later. My shift swung from low gear to high from that point on. I managed to text Ben, Gracie, and Sam a couple times, letting Ben know I'd meet him Thursday as planned and telling Gracie and Sam that I'd connect with them as soon as I got a minute.

My lack of sleep had me craving sugar. I met Jeffrey at eight a.m. at the Starbucks in Barnes & Noble. I was still sleep deprived after a large, smoked-butterscotch frap and two frosted cake pops, but I didn't plan on leaving without at least two new paperbacks.

Jeffrey pulled a list of addresses from his pocket. Smoothing the paper on the table, he pointed. "These three are in town, this one's closer to Ashland, and that one is … um, well …" He chuckled. "I'm not really sure."

Covering a yawn, I studied the list. "Have you looked at any of them yet?"

"No. Waiting for your recommendations."

I fought another yawn and lost. "This one is good." I pointed at the second on his list. "And so are these." I rubbed my neck while pointing to the fourth and fifth. Then I slid the paper back to him. "I'd avoid the other two."

"Are you all right?" He squinted at me, folded the paper, and returned it to his pocket.

"I had a busy shift. Didn't get much sleep."

"Kallie, you should've told me. We didn't need to meet."

"That's okay. It's probably a good idea you jump on these. They won't last long."

"Let's go." He stood and grabbed my pack. "You need to get home and sleep."

"Thanks. I think I will."

He walked out with me and watched me drive away, waving.

A rush of disappointment crashed over me. *So no new books? Fine. I'll come back later.*

I set my alarm for one since I'd be meeting Ben at two. I climbed under the covers and remembered nothing until the obnoxious buzz from my phone woke me a couple hours later.

◕◔

While eating string cheese and an apple, I changed into clean jeans and my *I survived the Kobayashi Maru* T-shirt. I opened the front door before Ben even knocked. Okay, I was watching for him. I chewed fast. "Hi," I said around my last bite. I swallowed. "I'm ready."

"Are your doors locked?"

"Yes." I smiled and nodded. "I even got one on the back-patio gate, like you suggested."

"Good." Ben gestured toward his unmarked car.

"Did you talk to Mrs. Whedon?" I buckled into the front passenger seat.

"Called her first thing Tuesday." He backed out of my driveway.

"What does she think? I mean, about what I do?"

He shrugged, stopped at the bottom of my street, and, after looking both ways, turned left. "She didn't seem to have any thoughts." He frowned and tipped his head. "In fact, she seemed quite interested—asked a lot of questions."

"Like?"

His frown deepened. "How accurate you were. Had you helped with many investigations. Stuff like that. I told her this was the first time the department has used your services and you're right on with your information so far."

"Did she say anything about Ariel or Ella?"

"No. Should she have?"

"I don't know. No. I guess not. I've just had them on my mind the last couple days."

Smiling at me, he entered the on-ramp to the freeway. "I'm sure they're fine." But his smile faltered, and his bright-green eyes darkened. He turned his attention to driving, glanced in the rearview mirror, and frowned. "We'll be there soon." His frown deepened.

"You okay, Ben?"

"I'm fine." He shrugged and repeated, "I'm sure Ariel and Ella are, too."

"Did Mrs. Whedon say anything else?"

His fingers gripped the steering wheel, knuckles white. "That's just it. She didn't ask about any progress toward identifying the body found in Eagle Point, or if we had any new information regarding the case at all."

Half an hour later, Ben turned up the curved gravel drive to the Whedons'. In the daylight, I noticed a llama and a miniature donkey in a corral next to the barn. They both stood at a feeder stuffed with hay, munching peacefully.

Well, that's a good sign.

Stopping at the top of the drive, Ben parked. "Let's go see Ella and Ariel." The sudden tension around his eyes was carried in his voice. Slipping out of his seat, he reached down and freed the strap holding his gun in the holster.

I scrambled out the passenger side. "Ben. What's wrong?"

"Nothing. Probably. But stay behind me." Hand on his gun, Ben took the steps onto the deck two at a time. He slowed when he reached the front door.

My words came in a raspy whisper. "What did you see?"

"Shhhh." Finger against his lips, he stood to one side of the door.

A soft wind sighed through the tree tops and faded to silence. No birds chirped. No small animals darted under the low brush. The day seemed to stop in the moment.

I glanced around. My gaze landed on a sheer curtain fluttering out an open window at the far end of the deck. "Ben." The low squeaking whisper never left my dry throat.

Ben tried the knob, and it turned in his hand. He pushed, and the heavy wooden door swung in a silent arc inward. Looking back at me, he mouthed, "Stay here."

I nodded, the movement almost undetectable, and wiped sweaty palms down my jeans as he disappeared inside.

I fought the urge to chase after him. A scene from the thriller movies I like to watch ran through my mind—the one where the girl stays outside and gets attacked after her boyfriend goes inside the big spooky house. "Why is it any safer out here?" My tongue stuck to the roof of my mouth. I worked at slowing my breathing. Gravel crunched behind me and I spun around, my heart lurching into an irregular cadence. Nothing there. Swallowing hard, I took a deep breath. "Get a grip, Kallie."

In an almost choreographed moment, Ben dashed outside as Ariel raced across the deck from the back of the house. His face tight with concern, Ben punched numbers into his phone.

Before Ariel could slam into my legs, I squatted and scooped the trembling dog into my arms. Caked dirt lined her wide eyes, and her matted fur was full of stickers.

"This is Detective Jacobson. Send all available units and a CSU to my coordinates. Contact Captain Granger. Let him know Mrs. Whedon and the two kids are gone." Ben ended the call and slipped his phone into his back pocket.

"Gone?" I clutched a trembling Ariel tighter.

Ben frowned. "What happened to Ariel? Is she okay?" Before I could answer, his gaze shifted to me and he nodded. "They're gone, and by the looks of the house, it's possible they were taken against their will." He motioned me forward. "Stay with me. Don't touch anything." He glanced at Ariel.

"I'm not putting her down. She's terrified." Straightening, I stared at him with as much determination as I could pull from my own fear. "I can hold her."

"Okay."

Following him into the house, I saw what he'd meant about "against their will." Glass from broken windows littered the entry's and living room's hardwood floors. In the kitchen, drawers pulled from cabinets lay on the tile at our feet. Their contents were scattered everywhere, mingling with jagged shards of dishes raked from the cupboards.

"Looks like they were looking for something," I said as I tucked a whining Ariel closer. "I wonder if they found it."

We circled through the dining room and down the hall, checking the bedrooms. A sudden quiet enveloped me as I stepped onto carpet, glass no longer crunching underfoot. Clothes spilled from open dresser drawers. Closet doors gaped, empty hangers askew. A blank space from the corner of each closet stood out with a significance I couldn't quite grasp.

In the master bedroom, I finally captured the idea flitting inside my brain. *Their suitcases are gone.* I stepped into the bathroom. Drawers hung open, rifled through in haste. Cold medicine, aspirin, and old makeup tubes lay strewn over the counter. "Ben? Could you open the medicine cabinet above the sink?"

Gloves on, he pulled the edge and revealed the small space.

Empty.

"I think they left on their own—in a hurry. But I believe they got out before whoever came in and trashed the place."

"Yeah. I think so, too." Ben turned to look at the dog relaxing into a doze in my arms. His forehead furrowed. "Why would they leave without taking Ariel?"

I bit at my lip. "Maybe they couldn't find her. Or maybe they left so fast." I leaned my face down to kiss the top of Ariel's head. "I don't know."

"If they left Ariel, what about Ella?"

I beat Ben to the deck, where an unsettled Ariel no longer dozed in my arms. I scanned the low brush, peering into the shadows.

Nothing.

"Ella. Come here, kitty," Ben called, voice shaking. He dashed off the deck, first searching the gravel driveway leading to the barn and then spinning around, head whipping back and forth.

"Ben," I called. "You'll only frighten her. Just calm down. If she's here, we'll find her."

Sirens sounded in the distance.

"That was fast." I focused my attention to the end of the road. Within seconds, a green-and-white cruiser turned up the drive, gravel spraying behind it.

"Probably in the area." Ben waited until the unit stopped and then met the officer as she climbed from her vehicle.

"Wilkens, start setting up a perimeter." Ben pointed to the residence and surrounding yard. "Everything." He gestured with a wave that encompassed a wide area.

"I'll sit in the car with Ariel."

Ben smiled at me. "Thanks."

ᏋᎤ

Warm sunshine, a cool breeze, and not much sleep was a triple whammy when it came to staying awake—that and my sugar high had worn off. I'd left the car door open and, with Ariel on my lap, gotten as comfortable as possible in the upright front seat. It didn't take much. I was vaguely aware of matching Ariel's soft snores in minutes. Mumbling, I allowed myself a *short* snooze—a quick power nap.

A gentle tap on my cheek followed by a light tickle across my nose brought me out of a deep sleep. A low rumble vibrated under my chin. I smiled. "Well, hello, Ella." I coaxed my lids open and saw Ella sitting on Ariel's back, her front paws just below my shoulders, staring at me with clear green eyes. I stroked her from head to tail. "I'm so glad you're okay."

Aware of movement in my peripheral vision, I noticed Ben about ten feet away.

Brow furrowing, his smile wavered. He mouthed, "What do I do? I don't want to scare her."

Continuing to pet the cat, I whispered, "Ella, there's Ben. He's your friend."

She glanced at him and then curled into a ball on top of a sleeping Ariel.

"It's okay. You can come over. They are both exhausted."

"Just them?" He stepped over and knelt at the open door. "I think you could use some sleep, too." His movements slow, he reached out to pet Ella.

She purred and arranged her head under his hand.

"I'm going to be here a while." He sighed and glanced back at the house. "I'll get someone to take you home." His focus on me, he asked, "What do we do with these two?"

"They can come home with me." I put my left arm around Ariel and used my right to pull Ella closer.

"You sure?"

"Yes. It'll give them time to calm down and me time to find out what they know. I don't work until Monday. They need some love and attention, along with food and rest."

His smile faded. "How long have they been on their own?"

"I think about two days. I'll know more later."

"I'll get a voucher from the department and have what you need sent to your place. You know—dishes, food, beds, whatever."

"Oh, can you see what they've been eating? It's hard on them to suddenly switch foods."

"I'll do that right now." Ben stood, still looking at me, and motioned to a uniformed officer. "Thank you, Kallie."

Chapter 11

As Ben promised, two boxes of supplies arrived a couple hours after the officer dropped me and my houseguests off—beds, toys, food, treats, and kitty litter. Perched on the back of the couch, Ella watched me unpack while Ariel insisted on sniffing each item and tossing around a few of the toys. "Ben did good, huh, guys?" After their dinners, my two new room-mates settled in, a purring Ella on my pillow and Ariel trotting behind my every move.

The evening brought rain drumming on the roof, large drops pattering against the windows. I changed into sweatpants and a long-sleeved T-shirt, grabbed a blanket, and dropped on the couch, Ariel next to me. I picked up the remote, and the TV blinked on. The breaking story of the missing Whedon family was dominating the news. The camera alternated between showing a distant shot of the deck, the front of the house, the police presence, and reporters standing before a backdrop of the barn. I didn't need or want to hear what they said and pressed mute.

"Well, it's not a secret anymore."

Ariel stirred at my voice. She raised her head and glanced at the large screen. Uninterested in the activity, she flopped back down with a long groaning sigh.

"Yeah. Me too." I found an old horror movie fest on a classic station and settled in, watching giant ants invade the tunnels under LA, until my phone vibrated against the side table.

"Sam, hi."

"Kallie, they're talking about you and the family that disappeared in the news. Are you okay?"

"I'm fine." I sat straight, throwing off the blanket. "What are they saying? And who's 'they'?"

"Some reporter's doing a live newscast. It's all about you communicating with animals and that you're helping the authorities with the case."

"Oh noooo." Eyes closed, I rubbed my forehead. "Who could have found that out? And why tell the news?" *It's the media circus Ben's boss feared.*

The phone buzzed in my ear. I glanced at the screen. "I gotta go. My mom's calling. I'll call you back."

"You better."

"Hi, Mom. What's up?"

For the next half hour, I did my best to calm my distraught mother. It wasn't an easy task since I wasn't pleased about being mentioned on several news channels either. After promising I'd call if I found out anything else, my calmer but far from happy mom said good night.

I considered going back to stay for a few days at Gracie's. But that meant uprooting Ariel and Ella again, and I didn't want to do that unless, *until*, it was necessary. "No." I shook my head. "Nothing's going to happen. No one knows where I live. Right? We'll be fine here. Won't we?" The memory of the knife through the cupcake box tightened a frown forming on my forehead. "But that was an isolated incident. I didn't have a lock on my back gate. Just kids messing around." I inhaled and then exhaled through pursed lips. "Sure. Just kids."

Untangling from the blanket, I got up and checked windows and doors one more time.

Ariel watched me, her head poking from under a fold of the cover I'd tossed over her. She didn't seem to mind the added warmth and concealment.

The porch light on the patio illuminated the area enough so I could see that the gate was locked. I flipped the switch, turning off the small bulb's radiance.

Shadows jumped as a gust of wind whipped branches and sent rain tapping against the glass. Pulse pounding, I backed up. Another gust rattled the door in its frame. I turned and dashed to the sofa where Ariel snoozed. Leaning over the back cushions, I peeked through the slats in the plantation shutters. The window overlooked the driveway and street. I checked right and left, my breath fogging the glass. Puddles shimmered on glossy pavement in the pale-yellow glow of streetlamps. Wind-blown leaves skittered across my lawn. Feeling foolish, I sighed. "There's nothing out there, Ariel. Stop being such a fraidy cat."

I remembered my promise to call Sam back and turned, adjusting the blanket. I picked up my phone from the side table and keyed in Sam's number.

Ariel kicked her back legs, stretched out, and snored softly.

Sam stayed on with me until my jangled nerves calmed and we laughed about how my sudden fame might be good for a raise at work or a friend request on Facebook from movie stars like Jason Momoa or Chris Pratt. Right.

At some point later, I woke up, the TV running the credits of *The Thing*—the original. *Darn. I missed it.* I scooped up Ariel and stumbled to bed, rousting a miffed Ella.

Ariel snuggled in at my side, and Ella took possession of the vacant pillow next to my head.

I lay there, a thick comforter enveloping me, and listened to the wind and rain. Sleep pulled at my eyelids. Thoughts became indistinguishable from the dreams that waited their turn from a blurry periphery, tugging at reality.

In a sudden jerk, Ariel sprang up, ears pricked. A muffled growl started deep in her chest.

My heart skipped, pulse jumping. That dozing comfortable lightness ripped away. Adrenaline coursed through me, my extremities tingling with the electric jolt of fear.

Ella's purring stopped. She slinked away, disappearing into the darkness.

Holding my breath, I listened. I couldn't hear anything except the moan of wind and incessant tap of rain. But Ariel had perceived something, and I trusted her instincts.

Turning my head in a slow, careful movement, I watched the red numbers of the clock on the nightstand blink to one fifty-seven.

Ariel's growl grew to a low bark, punctuated by quiet high-pitched whines.

I pulled my hand from under the covers and felt the top of the nightstand for my phone. It wasn't there. My heart thudded to a faster tempo. I must've left it on the end table next to the couch.

The soothing white-noise hum of the heat pump's fan clicked off, and the silence under that lulling drone seemed deafening.

A gust of wind screamed around the eaves. Branches scraped at the windows of my bedroom.

Raising my head, I saw a wan glow filtering down the hall from the stove light I'd left on in the kitchen. I slipped out from under the covers, bare feet hitting the carpet. Standing still, I listened. In a moment of bold decision, I hurried to the intersection of my bedroom door and the hall.

Ariel hopped off the bed and stayed at my heels.

Peering toward the kitchen, I watched dappled shadows caper across the living-room floor. Backlit by streetlights, the tree outside the front window had a few hardy leaves clinging to its limbs, creating a wind-driven dance like wraiths in the gloom.

Another click sounded, and the meager light shining from under the stove's hood died.

Breath catching in my throat, my attention focused on the weak illumination coming from outside. I stepped back, still staring toward the kitchen and living-room area, and pressed the light switch on the wall just inside the bedroom. Nothing. The power was out, but only in my house.

Looking at Ariel, I whispered, "I've got to get to my phone." Unsure whether I said this aloud for the dog's benefit or for mine, I nodded. "Yes, then call nine one one."

I always wondered why in thrillers when the character makes the decision to move, they creep down the hall or through the spooky woods at an agonizingly slow pace. Okay, fine. I get that it builds tension. Really, this only makes them an easier target. So I dashed instead, snatched my phone, and dropped into a crouch in front of the side table.

Ariel ran into my legs, steadied herself, and glanced up past the back of the couch to the plantation shutters.

Outside, a tall, solid shadow crossed the front window.

I clasped my hand over a gasp.

Her head low, Ariel growled.

"Shhhh." I ducked lower and pulled Ariel into a hug. "It's okay," I whispered. One elbow on the floor, I clutched the phone and with shaking fingers pressed the power button. The screen lit up, casting a bright radiance over the space where I tried to be invisible. Fumbling with the phone, I shoved it partway under Ariel and my arm. The light dimmed. I listened. There was no crack of breaking glass or thud of fists on wood—nothing but the sigh of wind and the *tap, tap, tap* of rain. I took in a shuddering breath. "Maybe it's only a tripped breaker. I'd need to go into the garage to check. Nope. Not happening." I watched the dancing leaf shadows on the floor beside me. "And that tall human-shaped shadow was, umm, was—"

Something crashed out back in my small patio, shattering on the concrete. A loud bang of wood striking wood followed.

"Okay, that's it." I pressed nine one one with my thumb, took a deep breath, and waited for the dispatcher to answer.

The first unit must have been right around the corner. The reflection of red and blue strobes colored the wall behind my TV, but no siren heralded the arrival.

Good. I stood, Ariel in my arms, and hurried to the front door.

After the second and third units showed, Ben dashed into the house wearing jeans and a sweatshirt, made eye contact with me where I sat at the kitchen table, and held up one finger. Hair mussed and wet from the rain, he strode to the French doors leading to the patio.

About five minutes later, he returned and shifted a kitchen chair to sit next to me.

"Sorry. I didn't mean to disturb you and to cause all this fuss." I grimaced. "But when the lights went out, and with the noises in back—"

"Kallie, I'm here because I want to be. You're not disturbing me."

"Thanks. So what's going on?" I glanced toward the patio where two officers stood, their flashlights cutting beams across the tall cedar fence.

"Someone smashed the lock on the patio gate and vandalized some of the potted plants. They also got into your garage through an unlocked window and shut your power off." Looking away, he took in a deep breath.

"And?" I leaned forward.

Ariel padded into the room, nails clicking on the hardwood. She sat between our chairs, her attention swiveling from me to Ben.

Taking a moment to pat her head, Ben finally met my gaze. "They spray-painted a knife on your front door."

My mouth dropped open, and it felt as though I'd been punched in the gut. "A what?" I jumped up and paced from the table to the sink. Everything around me blurred, the background voices of the police officers muted. *You heard him. They spray-painted a knife on your door. Just like the cupcakes.* I started out of the kitchen, toward the entry.

Ben blocked me, his hands on my shoulders. "You don't need to see it."

My tone harsh, I asked, "Why?" I closed my eyes. *Breathe. Just breathe.* "Sorry. There's more, isn't there? Tell me, Ben. Please."

He didn't respond.

"If you don't, I'll go see for myself."

"It's dripping red, into a puddle of red."

"You still think it's kids?" I ducked from under his hands and headed to the back of my house.

"Where are you going?" He followed, his footsteps muffled on the carpet.

"I need to find Ella."

Ariel's quick, soft padding trailed Ben.

"Good. Okay. Let's find her."

Chapter 12

I FOUND ELLA TUCKED BETWEEN two pairs of boots in the far right of my closet. She refused to leave her dark hiding place no matter how much I tried to coax her.

Kneeling at my side, Ben patted the floor in front of him. "Come on, Ella. It's okay." He patted his thigh. "Come on."

I swear Ella glared at him and frowned. That was it. I lost it. Yup, I laughed—a lot. After all the stress of the night, it felt good.

Ben sighed. "I know I'm not good at this. I haven't been around many cats. So teach me what to do." His brow wrinkled. "You said anyone could, uh, communicate with animals."

"Really? You know it takes time and practice. You can't be afraid to fail sometimes." I glanced at Ella. "And you're trying with a cat who has been through yet another trauma. Be prepared to get nothing." I adjusted to a cross-legged position.

Ben did the same. "I promise I have no expectations."

"Start with a few deep breaths in and out, slowly. Then close your eyes. Relax. Try to empty your mind."

I closed mine, inhaled, and visualized Ella going to sit on Ben's lap and him petting her. I also opened my mind so I could confirm what Ben saw in case he did get something.

Ariel sat against my back. The vision I got came from her. *The barn, the llama, and the mini donkey.*

I'll find out about them, I answered.

Ariel curled up, still touching me, and sent no more images.

"Well, I am getting something, but not like what I thought."

I opened my eyes. Ella sat on Ben's lap, purring softly. She adjusted her head under his hand so he would pet where *she* wanted. "Good job, Ben. She does like you."

"It's a start." He grinned. "And I like you too, Ella." His brow creased and the smile faded.

"What? *Did* you see something?"

"It's probably nothing. But I think I might have. Maybe just my own thoughts." His frown deepened. "Except it was the furthest thing from my mind."

"So tell me. I got a short vision. Maybe they're the same."

Looking at me sideways, Ben grimaced. "You wouldn't just say they are? You know, to be nice?"

Holding up my right hand, I nodded. "I wouldn't. I promise."

"Okay. Here goes." He let out a long breath. "I got a flash of the Whedon place. Actually, the barn."

"Anything else?"

He closed his eyes. "Hmm. The hay-holder thing." His head tipped. "The two animals—that little burro and alpaca." His lids popped open. "Probably just from my memories of the last day I was there." Lips turned up, he shrugged. "I see what you mean about adding your own visuals."

"Do you think they were yours?"

The creases on his forehead deepened. His attention snapped to Ariel, already snoring behind me. His gaze tracking to me, he asked, "Were they?"

"No. What do you think they mean?"

From the other end of the house, the low chatter from radios and hum of conversations trickled down the hall.

Staring into my closet while idly stroking Ella, Ben whispered, "Ariel's concerned about them."

"Yes." I stood. "Do you know where they are?"

His gaze unwavering, he said, "I'll find out first thing in the morning."

"You okay?" I patted his shoulder.

Ella in his arms, he stood. "I'm good."

I gestured for him to put Ella on the bed.

She headed straight for my pillow and snuggled in.

"Kallie." Ben took my hand and turned me to face him. "I'm sorry I ever doubted you."

❦

Several cups of coffee later, Ben and I sat at the kitchen table. The two remaining officers helped the crime-scene techs pack their equipment. It was almost eight, and I knew there would be no going back to bed. I thought maybe I'd catch a nap later. At seven I'd called the local handyman, Jake, to fix the gate and put in another lock—a stronger one. He had arrived minutes later and was tying up the last details.

My elderly next-door neighbor had showed up around six forty-five to clean my front door. I did appreciate his gesture to get things back to normal, but I also understood that this was his way to be helpful *and* find out what was going on at the same time. The door did look awesome when he finished. I saw homemade cupcakes in his future.

Ben stared into his empty mug. "I'm hungry." He glanced at me and tilted his head. "Want to get some breakfast?"

"Yes." I'd gotten dressed a short time after he got there, so I was ready to go. Half smirking, I asked, "Do you like pumpkin-spice pancakes?"

"Never had them. Sounds interesting."

"Oh, you have lived a sheltered life, Padawan. Let's go." I jumped up, grabbed my bag, and checked food bowls, water, and the whereabouts of my houseguests.

Jake tapped at the French doors.

Waving him in, I reached for my checkbook.

"All done, Kallie. Everything's locked up tight out there. They won't find it so easy to break in again." He continued through the house to the front door. "I'll send you a bill."

"Thanks, Jake." I did one last check of the locks and turned to Ben. "I'm ready."

Waiting for our pumpkin pancakes, bacon, and eggs, I asked, "Do you still think the first time was kids?"

Ben fingered the handle of his coffee cup. "No." He glanced out the window and then back to me. "I think this all has to do with what's happening or happened to the Whedons. I believe R and A is involved, but I'm not sure how. After what you told me, I looked up their LLC to get the owners' information." He shook his head. "They don't exist. No Mr. Smith. No Mr. Johnson. Not sure why no one checked into them further after Mr. Whedon disappeared." He looked at me, shook his head, and barked out a humorless laugh.

My phone conversation with Sam a couple days earlier came to me. I remembered her cousin's revelation regarding R and A's shady land acquisitions. "Have you talked with anyone in the county's planning department? And what about the office manager? Any record of who she is?"

"I read the original file." He pulled out a small pad and a pen. "Nothing about the office manager. There was a brief mention of someone talking with the planning department. Dead end."

"You might want to check again. I can get you the name of a planning employee who has a different take on R and A."

"A different take?"

Our food arrived. The sweet spicy, scent had my stomach growling and my mouth watering.

Buttering my pancakes, I continued, "Sam has a cousin who works there. He told her he thought their dealings are—were—a little off."

Ben sat back in his seat. "Why would Sam be talking to her cousin about this?"

I stopped mid-pour, syrup dripping from the lip of the small metal pitcher. "Oh, well, I told them what happened to me—what I'd found out. It's public knowledge." I shrugged. "They were curious. When they went to the office and found it empty, Sam asked her cousin about them."

Sighing, Ben stared at me, concern etched in the lines around his intense green eyes. "I appreciate the help …" The low timbre of his voice made it quite clear he was not happy. "But you have to stop. This is dangerous. Don't you see that now, Kallie?"

"Yes. I understand. We haven't done anything since." I sighed and nodded. "I'll let them know—no more investigating. But I still think you should talk to Sam's cousin." Groaning, I rubbed my eyes. "And my mom. She is going to freak."

"Let me talk to her—explain what we're doing." He took a bite.

"You'd do that?" I frowned. "And, what are *we* doing?"

"We the department, not we as in you." He stared at me. "Would you be willing to stay in your place with an officer on duty twenty-four seven? It may be a way to get a lead on what happened to the Whedons and find out who's behind this." He forked up another bite and stopped midway to his mouth. "These pancakes are really good."

Chapter 13

MOM OPENED THE DOOR AS we walked to the porch, her slight smile morphing to a wide grin when she saw Ben. "Come in, you two. I made coffee, and there's honey peach scones."

The aroma of a fresh pot and warm peaches wafted to the entry. I groaned inwardly, my stomach full of pancakes and bacon. Too bad. Her scones are amazing.

"Thanks, Mrs. Collins. Sounds good." Ben glanced at me, winked, and shrugged.

She escorted us through the foyer and into the kitchen. "Sit. I want to hear all about this break-in and what you plan on doing, officer."

"Oh, Mom, it's Detective Jacobson."

"Well, that's impressive," Mom gushed.

"Please, call me Ben." He held out her chair.

I hurried and sat, with Ben frowning at me. Okay, I didn't want him holding my chair. It's one of those awkward situations for me—I just don't know what to do.

Mom poured coffee.

Just what I didn't need. My head was buzzing, and I figured I could win

any race someone challenged me to. Well, not any, but I had already had a
massive amount of caffeine so far. I knew my crash wasn't going to be pretty.

Ben accepted the mug Mom handed him. "Kallie's house has been broken into twice in the last few days. We're not sure the incidents are related,
but it's a theory. I promise the department will do everything we can to find
out who's behind them."

Lips pursed, Mom stared at Ben. "Does this have something to do with
that body found in Eagle Point?"

"It's possible," he said as he nodded. "Probable."

She turned on me. "And this has to do with your *ability?*"

"Maybe." I shrugged, not wanting to tell her about my trip to R and A
under the ruse of employing their services.

"I see." Mom nodded. Her focus returned to Ben. "Will you be protecting my daughter?"

"Mom, I don't need protecting."

"Yes." Ben glanced at me. "There will be someone at her home all the
time."

"Good. I'm trusting you, Ben."

"I'll do my best, Mrs. Collins." He smiled. "Everyone involved will."

I hung my head and sighed. "Mom."

"Oh, Kallie, did you hear from Jeff?"

My head snapped up. "Mom," I whispered through clenched teeth.

"Weren't you helping him find a place?" She cast a quick peek in Ben's
direction.

"I'm just letting him know areas to stay away from. That's all. And,
yes, we met Thursday morning." I bit at my lip and glanced at Ben. Heat
flowed up my neck and into my face. *Great.* I stood, took my cup to the
sink, and dumped the coffee. Leaning against the island counter, I asked,
"Do you have any more questions, Mom? Ben—Detective Jacobson—has
work to do."

Her attention shifted to me, and I saw it—that twinkle in her blue eyes
and a slight smile turning her lips.

Ben dropped me at home, coming inside to check all the windows and doors.

Ariel greeted us with wiggles and wags. Ella sauntered in and sat in front of Ben. I gave him the bag of cat treats, I took the doggy snacks, and we handed out a few to each of them.

After patting Ella's head and scratching behind Ariel's ears, he smiled at me. "I'll call you later. The first shift, Officer Carter—I believe you met her the other day—will be here at three. Think of the teams as surveillance, like a stakeout—not just to *protect* you."

"Fine." The slight smirk twisting my lips dropped. "Thanks. Really."

"Glad to be of service." He grimaced. "Besides, I think we got you into this situation."

Still buzzing, I decided to make cupcakes for my neighbor. I called Gracie and then Sam, filling them in on the night's events while I blended chocolate batter, lined two pans with yellow, green, and pink papers, and popped them into the warmed oven.

Officer Carter—Tara—in street clothes, arrived in her own car. In her thirties, she reminded me of Zoe Saldana, except her black hair was short, framing her oval face and dark eyes. Her vehicle tucked in the garage, she did a quick check of the house, inside and out, and then settled into the recliner with a Brain Freeze from Dutch Bros and a book—a Sheriff Joanna Brady novel by J. A. Jance. Tara and I would get along just fine.

Cupcakes frosted and arranged in a square plastic container on the counter, my coffee high fading, I tottered to my room for a short nap. "Help yourself to cupcakes, or anything. There's coffee and reusable pods in the cabinet next to the Keurig. Not much in the fridge, but please, make yourself at home. And thanks, Tara."

"Go get some sleep. I'll be fine." She smiled and waved me away. "And you're welcome."

A light tapping roused me. Raising my head in the dark room, I looked at the glowing numbers on the clock. I bolted upright. "Seven o'clock? So much for a short nap." The tapping repeated.

Ariel beat me off the bed and stood at the closed door, tail wagging.

Raking a tangle of curls from my eyes, I opened the door and squinted at the light glaring from the living room and down the hall. "Sam. Hi."

"Sorry I woke you."

"It's okay. I didn't mean to sleep this long."

She pushed past me. "Good. We need to talk."

Whining and wiggling, Ariel demanded that Sam acknowledge her.

"Well, hello cutie." Sam dropped to her knees. "You must be Ariel."

Working my way around the two, I switched on a lamp on the nightstand and then flopped back down on the bed. Hand over my eyes, I whispered, "Give me a minute."

"And you must be Ella," Sam crooned.

The loud purring at the foot of my bed confirmed Sam's presumption.

Sitting straight with my back against the headboard, I pulled a pillow onto my lap. "What's up?"

Sam scooped Ariel into her arms and climbed on the bed next to me. "I never really got a chance to talk to you about my cousin."

"Your cousin?" My forehead creased.

Sam cuddled Ariel, kissing the top of her furry head. "The one that works at the planning department?" She rolled her eyes.

My head cleared. "Oh. Yeah." Ben's earlier lecture about being cautious flitted across my thoughts. His warnings didn't stick. Alert, eyes wide, I asked, "What did he tell you?"

"I don't want to explain twice. Comb your hair and wash your face. Let's go to Gracie's. She wants to know, too."

My stomach growled while I brushed my teeth, and I remembered I hadn't eaten since breakfast. Around a mouthful of cinnamon-y foam, I said, "I need to get something to eat."

"We'll stop for Chinese. I'm hungry, too, and Gracie will eat even if she's had dinner."

Tara sat at the kitchen table, an empty sandwich bag, a paper towel with a couple tortilla chips, and a cupcake paper in front of her. An iPad in her hands, she played a card game.

As I walked through the living-room, I noticed she'd closed the plantation shutter slats. Guess I should've thought about that. Can't have anyone looking in and seeing someone besides me at home. "I'm going out. Can I bring you anything?"

"No. Thanks. But if you could show me where you keep your spare blankets, I'll probably just watch a little TV and then get some sleep."

"You're welcome to the guest room."

"Thanks, but the couch is good. Is there anything I should know about your house guests?"

"Ella's good. She has everything she needs." I talked as I gathered blankets, pillows, and a clean pillowcase. "I'll take Ariel out, and she'll be fine until I get back. I won't be long."

Gracie hadn't eaten and was thrilled with the feast we'd brought.

Plates full, we settled in at her kitchen table.

I snapped my chopsticks apart and glanced at Sam. "Can you talk and eat?"

"Sure," she mumbled around a mouthful. Chewing, she pulled a notebook from her purse and flipped it open. "Okay. Mark, my cousin, told me that most of R and A's dealings appear to be legitimate." She ran a finger about a third of the way down the page. "Except there aren't very many. For a business like this to stay in the black, so he says, they'd need at least three times the clients they claim, maybe more."

Chopsticks hovering over cashew chicken, I frowned. "But if the company is new, wouldn't they expect some set timeframe for growth?"

Sam continued after wiping her mouth with a paper napkin. "That's what I asked." She shrugged. "Yeah, maybe, but he said that wasn't the real problem. The red flag moment for him was when he noticed that five of the twelve clients sold their property to them for next to nothing. They didn't contract with R and A to help them make the property more efficient or environmentally secure. They just sold their lands—and at a loss."

"What? How could they?" Gracie shook her head. "I don't get it. Were they older, or ..."

Sam looked at Gracie and then me and leaned across the table, her expression grave. "Mark dug a little deeper and believes *no* money actually changed hands."

"You mean they got the properties for free?" Gracie stared at Sam. "How is that possible? Isn't there paperwork, banks, and, yeah, title companies involved?"

Grinning, Sam sat back. "You'd think. That's where this gets really interesting. Mark said the forms from the title companies appeared legitimate except for one thing."

"Don't most of those papers need to be notarized?" I stirred sweet and sour into my cashew chicken.

"Exactly." Sam nodded, her brown eyes wide and bright with excitement. "But, get this, the same notary was used in all five cases, and due to *health of signatory*, the papers were signed outside of the *five different* title companies used."

"What about banks? There had to be checks and money deposited, didn't there?" Gracie popped the tab on a Dr. Pepper and took a drink.

"I asked Mark about that. He said R and A could write a check. Then that gets held to make sure it's good. Once it clears and all the legal paperwork regarding property transfer is complete, the check is delivered to the payee."

Sam had my full attention. "So money did change hands. Right?"

Chewing, Sam smirked. "Looks that way, doesn't it? Mark still had doubts, so he checked further. He called the title companies and said he needed more information about how the funds were delivered, to finish up on his end. Since he did work for the county, and what he wanted to know wasn't personal, the receptionists told him a delivery service was used and a signature of receipt required." She shook her head. "The same delivery company was requested by each of the payees."

"Uh-oh," Gracie whispered. "Bet the title companies didn't know that little bit of information. Had R and A used the same title company for all the transactions, the land transfers would have screamed scam."

"Yeah." Sam nodded. "How convenient."

"How did they get signatures on delivery?" My mind bounced this information around—how simple yet devious at the same time.

Sam shrugged. "Who knows? Some items do require one. Most wouldn't question having to sign for something delivered to their door. If the delivery people, or, say, one specific person, were in on the con, or even just getting paid to make a switch, they'd only have to substitute the check with something else." She nodded, the gesture more for herself than Gracie or me. "It could have been a package from Amazon or flowers or chocolate dipped fruit, and bingo—R and A has their check back *and* the title to the land."

"Do you think they even talked to the people about their property? For any reason? Selling or improving? I mean, can't signatures be checked?" I bit at my lip, still considering the logistics of this and what R and A might gain from this scam.

"I'm sure they had to at some point." Sam set her fork down and reached into her pack. "Mark did something he shouldn't have and will deny any knowledge if it ever comes up." She tapped the notepad. "I have the five names and addresses of the people Mark believes were taken advantage of. He'll check for more, but he said he can only do so much. He's worried his snooping might come to the attention of his supervisor." Glancing sideways at us, Sam smirked. "He can't look into these cases any further, but we can."

My frown deepened. "What is happening with the land? Are any of the lots for sale? That would be easy enough to check. Why else would they take over the properties if not to sell for a big profit? What about telling the cops? Could Mark go to the authorities?"

"Mark pretty much forgot until I asked him about R and A the other day. After that first detective showed up at the county office asking about Mr. Whedon and R and A several months ago, he figured it was taken care of." Sam tipped her head, eyebrows raised. "He hasn't seen any more come through planning connected to R and A since." She shrugged one shoulder. "He thought the issue was over."

"Several months?" I bit at my lip. "Do you know when the detective was there?"

Sam picked up the pad and scanned the page. "Hmmm. Mark thinks maybe mid-August."

"Okay. Definitely *after* Mr. Whedon's disappearance in July." I turned and faced Sam. "Did Mark say who the detective was and which employee he talked to?"

Shaking her head, Sam dropped the pad and picked up her fork. "I guess I could ask. No guarantee he'll know."

"The county offices are closed until Monday. But that doesn't mean we can't find out some stuff off the computer." I smiled and adjusted my chopsticks. "But let's eat first."

My phone rang a few minutes later. "By the way," I said, speaking fast, "Ben doesn't want us snooping around anymore. Because it might be dangerous. I told him I'd tell you."

Gracie smiled. "Tell *Ben* you mentioned it, if he asks."

Nodding, Sam shrugged.

I accepted the call. "Hi, Ben. Any news on who broke into my house?"

"No. This could take some time, but I hope having surveillance at your place will pay off, quickly. And, by the way, where are you?" He sighed. "Never mind. You don't have to tell me."

"That's okay. I'm at Gracie's with Sam. We're having dinner. I won't be gone long."

"You aren't under house arrest, Kallie. You can come and go as you please. Just leave the detective work to me."

"Of course. And I told Sam and Gracie what you said, about this being dangerous."

"She did," Sam yelled.

"Yup, she told us," Gracie added.

"Tell them thanks. I'll talk to you again tomorrow."

"Bye, Ben. Get some sleep."

"I plan on it." He chuckled. "Good night, Kallie."

The connection ended.

"Ben says thanks."

"He's welcome. Now, let's get back to it." Gracie took her laptop off the kitchen counter and opened it.

An hour later, and after two cupcakes each, all we'd found out was that the properties in question were very rural—primitive, even. There was no power or other utilities—just old out-buildings or dilapidated farmhouses.

Fingers drumming the table, Gracie sighed. "Well, if they're thinking of having a haunted-house attraction, it's a little late."

"They haven't been listed for sale," Sam said, arms crossed. "What are they waiting for?"

"Maybe we should go at this from another angle." I pointed at the laptop. "Sam, look up previous owners—the names Mark gave us. Let's check them out."

The first, a Mr. and Mrs. J. P. Adams, resided at an expensive retirement home in Medford.

I glanced at Sam and then Gracie. "How about we take cupcakes to the Adamses tomorrow?"

"I'm free." Gracie nodded. "Sounds like a solid plan."

"You mean, just walk in and ask to talk with them?" Sam paled. "Won't they question why we're visiting two people we don't even know?"

Thinking about this, I said, "We'll be honest—tell whoever asks, and especially the Adamses, why we're there." I looked at Sam. "You don't have to go if it makes you uncomfortable."

"No. I'll go. This is kinda exciting." Sam shivered. "I'm in. But I can't go until Sunday. My mom bought the whole family tickets to go see Macbeth at the Shakespeare Festival on Saturday."

Chapter 14

ON SUNDAY, SERGEANT CRAIG BLAKE showed up for stakeout duty just before ten. I walked Ariel, took a half dozen cupcakes to my neighbor, and, after a shower, met Sam and Gracie for a late breakfast in town.

I slid into the booth next to Gracie. "I think homemade treats might not be such a good idea. I mean, like you said Sam, Mr. and Mrs. Adams don't know us. But what about from a bakery in a taped box?"

"Is there one open today? It's Sunday." Sam held her coffee cup up for the waitress.

"Oooo, there's the one at the south end of town. They have great baked stuff." Gracie added cream to her mug.

"I know that place." I picked up the menu and decided—lingonberry crepes, and, yes, bacon.

Afterwards, we piled into Sam's car and headed to our first stop. We decided on cookies instead of cupcakes and then went to visit Mr. and Mrs. Adams.

Sam parked in front of the two-story building in the area designated for visitors. She glanced at me in the rearview mirror. "You sure this is okay?"

"Sam, do you feel like we're doing anything illegal?" I released the seat belt holding me.

"Well ..." She grimaced. "I guess not."

"We'll stop at the front desk and let them know who we are and why we're here. If they say no ..." I shrugged. "That's it. We'll leave."

Blowing out a long breath, she nodded. "Okay."

I led the way into the luxurious lobby, holding the door open for my friends, and we walked to the reception desk.

Leaning over the tall counter, I made eye contact with the young woman. "Hi. I was wondering if my friends and I could talk to Mr. and Mrs. J. P. Adams?"

She glanced at Sam and Gracie and then focused her attention on me. "Are you family?"

"Well, no—"

"Friends of the family?"

"No."

"Why do you want to see them then?"

Sam let out a quiet squeak.

The truth.

"My name is Dr. Kallie Collins. I don't know them, but I have some questions about a property they're associated with on Madrone Canyon Road. I'm concerned someone might have tried to take advantage of them. Before I pursue this any further or contact the authorities, I'd like to talk to them and get their story."

Glaring at me, her eyes narrowed. "Are you the animal psychic from the news?"

"Yes and no. That's me, but this has nothing to do with psychic abilities. It's more like empathy, or maybe a—"

"Kallie," Gracie whispered and stepped forward. "Hi. I'm Gracie. Could we leave a message with our numbers for Mr. and Mrs. Adams? If they want to talk to us, they can call."

"No." She frowned. "I mean, that won't work." Blowing out a long sigh, she tapped at the keys on her computer and glanced at the screen. "There's no notation saying they can't have visitors. I'm just glad someone is finally looking into what that Mr. Johnson tried to talk them into." She shook her head. "I can't imagine a housing development on land so far from town would ever do well. I contacted a distant relative from Washington—DC, not state—though I'm not sure they ever followed up. When Johnson stopped showing up, I assumed the matter was closed." Her shoulders drooped and she stared at the three of us. "They're a sweet couple, just … Well, you'll see. Room two thirty-seven." Pointing to the elevator, she offered a weak smile. "Good luck."

"Thanks." I waved at Sam and Gracie to follow me.

Once inside, the second-floor button pushed, Gracie asked, "Good luck? That doesn't sound encouraging."

"Yeah," Sam chimed in. "What do you think she meant by that?"

I shrugged. "Guess we'll find out." The doors opened and we stepped into a wide, colorful hallway. Turning right, I followed the room numbers on the wall.

Their room was on the left, and I stood in front of the door, my hand poised in the air.

"Wait," Sam squeaked. "What if they're napping?"

"I'll knock quietly."

"But if they don't hear well, they may not know someone's knocking." Gracie hitched her purse back over her shoulder, stepped forward, and—

The door swung open. A white-haired man, at least six feet tall and lean, stood grinning at us. "Are you going to stand out there gabbing at each other all morning, or you coming in?" He motioned us into the apartment, bright sunshine streaming in the large living-area window. "The front desk called. Said you were coming up for a visit. What's that?" He pointed to the bakery box I held.

"Oh. We brought you cookies." I held them out to him. "Hope you like chocolate chip."

"Indeed I do. My favorite. Thanks." He took them and smiled. "Good bakery. Used to go there when I was still driving." He shuffled to a recliner and lowered himself to the padded seat, groaning out a long sigh. "Eva," he called. "Our company's here." He kept glancing at me, his brow wrinkled.

Gesturing toward a long couch, he said, "Sit." He tossed a wave at a re-cliner covered by a colorful, flowery throw next to his. "Eva sits here."

A *scuff, clunk, scuff, clunk* sounded from the hall. "What, John?" Eva, ambling behind a walker, entered the living room. "Oh. We have company. Are these Linda's daughters?"

So the J was for John.

"Linda has sons, and they have daughters. So they'd be Linda's grand-daughters." He closed his eyes and shook his head. "But, no, they aren't Linda's."

"Hello, Mrs. Adams." I turned to Mr. Adams and as he stared at me, his frown deepened. "My name is Kallie Collins, and these are my friends Sam, uh, Samantha Griffin and Gracie Parker. I'd like to ask some questions about your property off Madrone Canyon Road."

Eva pushed her walker to the flowery recliner and settled into the seat. She tipped her head back, eyes closed. "That was left to John by his great uncle over forty years ago. He didn't have any children of his own." She sighed and glanced at her husband. "He loved you so much."

John nodded slowly. His stare seemed distant, as though he were look-ing into the past. He straightened, back in the present. "Well, all I can tell you is it's pretty rural out there. No power, no water—nothing."

"No, John. There is a well. But that was a long time ago. Probably dry and filled in by now." Eva nodded, staring at the carpet.

"So you still own the land?" I leaned forward, closer to John.

"Sure do." He held up a finger. "I did talk to some fella a few months back about grazing rights or the possibility of developing the site for some-thing. He never asked to buy it. Just wanted to help me—well, him and me—make some kind of income off it. Told him I was too old to start a project like that. That young fella kept coming back, trying to talk me into letting them do all the work for me. Said all I'd have to do was cash the checks every month." He scowled. "I still wasn't interested. I knew what it would take to make that land livable. Getting power out that far alone would cost more than the land's worth."

"Did you sign anything?" I bit at my lip. "Like any proposals or bids?"

"No." His brow wrinkled. "But I did sign some papers allowing the county to give that fella the assessor's plot maps, boundary lines, and egress points. Since I never heard from him after that, I figured he'd checked into the property and realized the cost wouldn't be worth his time."

My pulse quickened, anger churning. There it was. That's how R and A got his signature. You don't need permission for this information. It's public record. They took advantage of this kind old man's trust and seized control of property that's been in his family for generations.

"Do you remember the man's name or the company he worked for?" Gracie scooted forward, sitting on the edge of her seat.

John pursed his lips and gazed at the ceiling. "Hmmm. Let me think." He chuckled. "You know, if you asked me anything about my life twenty, thirty, even forty years ago, I'd give you an answer in a heartbeat. But honestly, I can't remember much about the last year or two. I can't even tell you what I had for breakfast."

"That's okay, Mr. Adams." I smiled. "Did this man give you any copies or a business card?"

Staring at me, he shook his head. "Not sure. Maybe. If he did, don't know what I did with it." His gaze lingered on me. "You look familiar. Are you Colleen's daughter?"

"No. My mother's name is Bridget. But my grandmother's name is Colleen."

"Colleen O'Shea?"

"Yes. Did you know her?"

John turned to Eva and took her hand. "Eva, honey, this young lady is Colleen's granddaughter."

"Colleen?" Eva stared at me and her eyes widened. "Oh my. You look just like her."

"That's what I hear." Heat rose up my neck and into my cheeks.

"We met your grandparents right after we got married. They were our neighbors at the first house we bought in town, on Oak Street." John smiled at the memory.

"I remember that house, and the big backyard."

"We didn't stay in that place long," he mused. "But we remained friends with your grandparents for many years." He glanced at Sam and Gracie.

"I'm sorry I couldn't help. Leave me your number—In case I do remember something. Not promising anything, but you never know." He tipped his head and grinned.

I jotted mine on a notepad from a table between their chairs. "Thank you for talking to us." I followed Gracie and Sam to the door.

"It was nice to see you again, Colleen." Eva waved and smiled.

"Good to see you, too. Goodbye."

Breaking the tape on the bakery box, John said, "And thanks for the cookies."

In the elevator, we looked at each other.

"How could anyone take advantage of such nice people?" Sam seethed, her tone low with irritation.

"Because they *are* nice—and trusting." Gracie stared at the floor with her arms crossed, holding back her outrage.

"Maybe we can do something—get their property back even." I pressed the lobby button on the elevator panel.

"How?" Sam frowned and watched the lights showing the floor change as we descended.

"Yeah. How? We can't prove Mr. Adams didn't know he was selling the property." Gracie shook her head. "He just can't remember well enough to fight it in court." She glanced sideways at me. "They knew your grand-parents, Kallie. You okay?"

"I'm fine—mad but fine." I stared at the floor. "Kinda makes this feel personal for me, though." With a new resolve, I gathered my emotions. Facing forward, I waited for the elevator doors to slide open. "There are four more names on the list your cousin gave us. We should check them out—get their stories." A chime sounded and the doors glided apart. "And find out what, if anything, is going on at the property on Madrone Canyon."

"You mean actually go there? When?" Sam asked, her voice quivering.

I shrugged. "Why not right now?"

"I was afraid you were going to say that." Sam lumbered out and down the hall behind Gracie and me, mumbling, "I've got a bad feeling about this."

I set the address in my phone's GPS, and Sam drove. A little over half an hour later, we turned up a gravel road lined by thick brush.

"Does this look, well, recently used?" Sam peered over the steering wheel.

Riding shotgun, I looked up from my phone. "Um, yeah. It kinda does. I mean, I didn't expect gravel. Mud maybe. And the gravel looks recent, like it hasn't been here long."

From the back, Gracie reported, "In spots, there are fresh tire tracks on the muddy shoulder."

"Okay. Find a place to pull over. No, wait. According to the GPS, there should be a side road ahead on the left. Turn in there and park so the car isn't visible from this road. We'll walk the rest of the way. The property's only a half mile from the main road turnoff."

"Stealth-mode time?" Gracie's tone buzzed with excitement.

"I think that might be a good idea. There," I called, pointing forward and to the left. A narrow dirt trail, just wide enough for a small car, wound into the dense undergrowth and around tall pines and cedars.

Sam didn't have to drive far on the path before the gravel road disappeared from view.

"Perfect. Okay, let's remember where we hid the car." I unbuckled and tucked my phone in my pack.

"Hid?" Sam took her time shutting off the engine.

From behind, Gracie patted Sam's shoulder. "Parked, Sam. Right, Kallie?"

"Oh, yeah. Parked." I opened the door and climbed out. Bending over, I glanced at Sam through the opening. "It's all good. Come on. We have a couple hours before the sun drops below the mountains and the light starts to fade."

"You mean we could be out here in the dark?" Sam joined me and scanned the forest. "There's bears up here, and cougars, right?"

"Don't worry, Sam. Kallie can talk to them. They'll leave us alone." Gracie took her cell phone and held it up. "Okay, everyone. Silence your phone."

"Good idea. Nice thinking, Gracie." I followed her lead.

"You guys are scaring me." The expression on Sam's face would have been comical if the situation wasn't actually a little scary.

I walked to the front of the car and pulled Sam's purple knit cap low over her long blond hair. "It's okay. Really. We'll walk in, see the place is abandoned, and walk out. Be back here in an hour—probably less."

"Promise?" Sam locked the car and put the keys in her pocket.

Gracie wound her arm through Sam's and tugged. "Promise. Let's go." She glanced back at me. "Should we walk on the road?"

Shrugging one shoulder, I nodded. "It'll be faster. If we hear someone coming, we'll have plenty of time to get off the road."

"To hide?" Sam squeaked.

I caught up to my friends. "We're fine, Sam."

Beams of sunlight lit our way. Birds chirped in gently swaying branches. The scent of recent rain mixed with the spicy aroma of pine and cedar.

"Say 'knock, knock,' Kallie." Gracie grinned.

Rolling my eyes, I groaned. "I don't know any knock, knock jokes. How's that going to work?"

"Just say it," Gracie pleaded.

"Fine. Knock, knock."

Grinning, Gracie chuckled. "Come in."

"Okay, that was kinda funny." I smiled.

Sam relaxed, laughing at more of the silly jokes. I think Gracie said them to ease her own nervousness as well.

The road ahead continued uphill at a gentle slope—an easy walk, with slight turns right and left. Trees crowded the berm, limbs hanging low and brushing the ground with the gentle breeze.

"Shhhh." I stopped. "Did you hear that?"

"What?" Sam grabbed my arm, her gaze darting down the road.

Finger to my lips, I listened. *Did I hear something?*

Gracie looked up, spinning in a slow circle. "Just the wind in the trees," she whispered.

A low rumble sounded from ahead.

"Okay. That I heard." Sam's grasp on my arm tightened.

"Let's get off the road." I started to move right as Gracie headed left.

Sam squealed. "Which way?"

"It doesn't matter." I gripped the sleeve of Sam's coat and followed Gracie.

The rumbling grew—a vehicle, probably a truck, moving slow.

We pushed through brush and low limbs and stood next to the thick trunk of a fir tree, hidden by dense boughs.

Gravel crunched, and the growl of an approaching engine was unmistakable.

"Get down," I whispered in a harsh rasp.

We hit the ground and peeked through entwined branches of needle leaves.

From my angle, I couldn't see any passengers in the big white truck— just wide tires and muddy side panels.

Staying inside the safety of the trees, we waited until the rumble faded and disappeared.

Beside me, Sam let out a slow breath. "Can we go home now?"

"We're so close." I frowned and glanced at Gracie. "Do you want to go?"

"I say we finish this." Gracie stood, brushing dead needles from her jeans.

Keeping my voice level, I suggested, "We have no idea who that was. Maybe hunters. It is deer season."

Gracie pushed out onto the road. "You're right. Just because there was a truck out here, in the middle of nowhere, doesn't mean it has anything to do with the Adamses' property or R and A or dead bodies or missing people."

Hands on hips, I glared at Gracie. "Really?"

Gracie stared back at me with her eyebrows raised. "Tell me that didn't freak you out a little."

Sam raised her arm and waved her hand. "I'll admit it."

"Okay. Maybe." I couldn't stop the grin tugging at my lips. "But also kinda exciting."

Grabbing Sam's hand and then mine, Gracie started forward. "I know."

"I repeat, I have a bad feeling about this," Sam groaned.

"We'll be careful now that we know there are people out here." My grin widened. "Besides, we aren't doing anything wrong."

Gracie chuckled. "Um, didn't you tell Ben you'd stop playing Nancy Drew? What do you think he's going to say about this?"

"Kinsey Millhone," I mumbled.

"What?" Gracie stared at me.

Squaring my shoulders, I said, "Kinsey Millhone, not Nancy Drew. And that was before I met John and Eva Adams. Like I said, this is personal now."

Chapter 15

GRAVEL CRUNCHING UNDER OUR FEET, we trudged up the sloping road.

"Do you really think they were just hunters?" Sam whispered. Her clutch on my hand had my fingers tingling.

"Sure." I nodded. "What else?"

The chirping in the trees quieted. Wind stilled. An eerie silence accompanied lengthening afternoon shadows.

"Is it getting dark?" Gracie glanced at the sunlit treetops.

"No. Sun's just going below the mountain ridges." I checked the time. "We still have over two hours before it sets."

The road took a sweeping right to a narrow drive. What remained of a small cabin, roof caved in and graying and splintered walls leaning in on each other, stood next to a new barn of unpainted wood and a shiny tin roof. Two wide swinging doors at the front were closed with a padlocked chain through metal handles. Fresh tire tracks lined the mud, but no vehicles were present.

"That is definitely not abandoned." Gracie took a few steps toward the side of the road and the closest tree cover.

"Nope, not deserted," I agreed.

From where we stood, a clearing of maybe thirty yards separated us from the barn. I listened. There was nothing—not even birdsong or sigh of wind. "I'm taking a look." I glanced at Sam and Gracie. "You can stay here if you want." I got a simultaneous "No" from Gracie and a weak "Okay" from Sam.

The crack of a rifle in the distance echoed around us. Another sharp report bounced along the canyon walls.

Sam stared at Gracie. "Well, I'm not staying here alone."

"Let's go, then." Gracie stepped out of the trees, Sam behind her.

I ran in a silent half crouch until I flattened myself against the wooden side of the barn, as though I were some kind of special ops soldier on a mission. *I watch way too much TV.* The scent of freshly sawed wood and churned earth tickled my nostrils.

Beside me, Sam panted. "What now?"

"Do you see a window?"

"No." Gracie pointed. "Maybe in the back?"

We shuffled side by side, keeping close to the rough-hewn wood. I peeked around the edge and, seeing no one, nodded. Two small high windows flanked a door in the center of the rear wall.

I hurried to the farthest and, standing on tiptoes, tried to see inside. A dark tint covered the panes.

"Kallie," Gracie whispered, gesturing me to where she and Sam stood. "There's something like paint on the glass, but it's peeling on the bottom corner. I can't see much. It's pretty dark in there, but I don't know. Tables? You look."

Fingers gripping the sill, I peered through a ragged two-inch square and tried to make sense of what I saw. A row of empty tables lined one side, and scattered boxes the size you might get boots in littered the dirt floor. I couldn't see any higher than the tabletops. The edge of the tinted window didn't allow more of a view. Letting go, I dropped down. "Yeah. I saw tables and lots of shoe or boot boxes." I sidestepped to the door and, with care, pulled the handle. It didn't budge. I yanked harder. Nothing. "Locked from the inside."

Sam grimaced. "Have they been there awhile? Maybe someone's storing their stuff."

I shook my head. "Didn't look old—no dust or dirt on the tabletops." I chuffed. "They actually looked really clean. So did the boxes."

The wind picked up, whistling under the broad eaves of the barn.

I pulled the hood over my head and tucked wind-blown curls up under the soft cloth.

"So what are they doing?" Gracie zipped her coat.

I glanced at the locked door. "Good question."

"Should we call the police?" Sam crossed her arms and glanced around, focusing on the line of trees and brush twenty or more feet from where we stood.

I considered her suggestion. "And tell them what? We need more information about the other properties before we can prove or even question what R and A is up to here."

"Yeah. I agree. I mean, tables and boxes? Not much to go on." Gracie shook her head. Her short dark hair drifted in the breeze, flitting across her wide hazel eyes. She brushed the strands away and tipped her head. "Too bad we can't get inside." Frowning, she dashed past the second window and peered around the far corner of the barn. She pulled back and trotted over to us. "No windows or doors there."

I heard the low rumble of an engine a fraction of a second before Gracie and Sam.

"They're coming back," Sam shrieked and ran to the tree line behind the barn.

Gracie and I followed, ducking under low limbs and into shadows.

Two vehicles appeared—the same white truck from earlier and a van, dark blue or maybe black.

Black like the one in the vision I saw at the Whedons'?

They both pulled out of my line of sight to the front of the barn. I side crept through the low branches and brush, trying to get a look.

"Kallie," Gracie whispered. "What are you doing? Get back here."

Holding a finger to my lips, I mouthed, "I want to see who they are."

"Wait for us," Sam whispered. "We're coming with you." She moved one small step at a time, watching the barn between her slow advance toward me.

I checked the route I'd need to get a clear view. A dry ditch about two feet deep and three feet wide and littered with small boulders ran to my right. The sloping banks and at least four feet beyond on both sides were scrubbed clean of brush. To cross, we'd need to follow the tree line down and away from the barn until we could pass without being seen. By the time we'd come back up, hidden among the trees and bushes, they'd be in the barn and out of sight. Waiting until they came out again, if they did emerge any time soon, wasn't something I was willing to wait for.

Gracie settled in next to me. "Let's go. We should get out of here and head to the car."

"Please, Kallie," Sam pleaded. "I've had enough excitement for one day."

"Yes. I agree. Follow me." I headed parallel to the ditch, staying in the trees and crossing when I could no longer see the barn. Scrambling up the opposite bank, I reentered the woods.

"Where are you going?" Gracie asked between breaths. "Can you find your way to the car?"

I looked back, smiled, and nodded. "Easy." My smile faded. "But we need to hurry. It's going to get dark fast." I pushed a pine bough away and froze.

I could hear men's voices. Loud. Yelling. All talking at once.

Craning her neck, Gracie asked, "What are they saying?"

"I can't tell." I frowned. "It's all jumbled."

"They're arguing about a late shipment and money. Someone has to pay for losses?"

Gracie and I both turned to look at Sam.

I stared at her, impressed. "You can understand what they're yelling about?"

"Yeah. They all have different tones. I just have to separate which I want to listen to and, uh, yeah. Some of it, anyway."

They started up again, louder and angrier.

I took Sam's shoulder. "What are they saying?"

Grimacing, Sam tipped her head. "No one wants to explain to Hawk about why the shipment is late." She wrinkled her nose. "He won't be happy. His people, the ones he reports to, aren't exactly the understanding kind." Shaking her head, she shut her eyes. "Um, something about a product and it going bad?"

The voices faded, and a door slammed.

Sighing, Sam shrugged. "That's all I got."

"Okay. Let's get out of here." I led the way, and we made it with daylight to spare.

After we got on the highway, Gracie asked, "So what do you think their *product* is?"

Sam glanced in the rearview mirror. "Drugs?"

"Can that go bad?" Gracie's phone lit up in the back. "No signal yet."

Tapping the steering wheel, Sam frowned. "I may have got that part a little mixed up. Maybe they said the product *is* bad? Can be bad?" She blew out a breath between pursed lips. "Two had accents. Reminded me a little of Arnold Schwarzenegger." She shook her head. "But not exactly."

"It doesn't make sense. What are they doing in such secrecy that *doesn't* have to do with drugs?" Gracie tapped my shoulder from behind. "What do you think, Kallie? Did you pick up anything while we were out there?"

"Nothing. It was all quiet. But then, I wasn't exactly opening myself for the visions of any animals around willing to share." I looked at Gracie and grinned.

"Are you going to tell Ben?" Sam flipped on the headlights.

"No. Not really anything to tell him."

Chapter 16

SAM DROPPED ME OFF AT home. Craig had a football game on, the volume low. Ella was again curled up on my pillows, so I took a wiggling Ariel for a long walk. Streetlamps lit long bands of the sidewalk, and soft yellow porchlights shone from front doors like welcoming little beacons. "I think it's time you, me, and Ella have a chat."

Snuffling, Ariel looked at me.

The breeze chased dancing leaves across the street. I love this time of year—the scent of rain and soil with just a hint of wood smoke, the crisp air, and warm sunny days.

"I know. You told me a lot already, but maybe there's more. If we could put our heads together and sort out what you saw ... I don't know. Maybe there's nothing. But we should try. And I haven't talked to Ella yet at all."

Coming around the last corner, a strange truck pulled away from the curb in front of my house. I stepped back into the shadows of a tree until it drove by.

I hurried into the entry and unhooked the leash.

Closing the refrigerator door, Craig turned with a soda in his hand. "Did you have a nice walk?"

"Yeah." I frowned. "Who was just here?"

He shook his head. "No one. Why?"

"It's probably nothing. I saw a truck in front." I gestured toward the street.

Setting the soda down, Craig said, "Stay here." He pulled his gun from a shoulder holster and went out through the access to the garage.

I waited, pressed against the kitchen wall.

After ten minutes, the door connecting the laundry-room hall and garage opened. Craig checked all the rooms inside and then returned to the kitchen. His gun back in its holster, he shrugged. "Nothing looks disturbed. No one's hanging around outside. I think it's okay."

"Thanks. Well, see you in the morning." I started toward my bedroom but turned to Craig once more. "Do you need anything?"

He picked up his soda. "I'm fine. My wife packed an ice chest for me. The pillows and blankets are on the couch, and"—he smiled—"there's another game in a few minutes. I'm all set."

"I have a twelve-hour shift tomorrow." I looked at Ariel, her ears pricked and tail wagging. "I'll take her with me. Ella will be fine here. She's pretty independent."

In my room, Ariel jumped on the bed and snuggled in next to Ella.

Wind sighed along the eaves, the sound calming.

My phone vibrated in my pocket. "Hi, Ben. How's it going?"

"It's good. What were you up to today?"

"Me? Nothing much." My mouth went dry. I cleared the squeak from my voice. "Just hanging out with Sam and Gracie."

"Sounds like trouble." He chuckled.

"No trouble." I squawked out a nervous laugh. "Sam won't let me."

"Remind me to thank her." A chair squeaked. "The department wants to continue our presence at your place a few more days. Is that okay? They're still hoping someone will show and we can get answers."

"Sure. I hardly know they're here."

"You're working the next three days, right?"

"Yeah. Three twelves, then off for two."

"Just do your regular routine. And by the way, Craig loves your big screen."

This time my laugh was natural. "I'm glad. I do appreciate all they're doing. Thanks, Ben."

"Get some sleep. I'll talk to you tomorrow. Bye."

"Bye." I tossed my phone on the bed, guilt twisting my expression. Sam, Gracie and I were together, so I hadn't really lied. Dropping down, I sighed. "Would you have told him if he asked? Of course. But he didn't. And nothing happened." Switching on the TV, I searched for something upbeat to watch and settled on a *Golden Girls* marathon.

Craig let me know that his relief would be there at nine. Grinning, he assured me he'd be back soon. I guess he did really like the TV.

I packed food, treats, toys, and a blanket for Ariel, made sure Ella's bowls were full and her litter box was empty, and left for work in the dark. A few minutes later, Ariel and I pushed through the front doors of the hospital.

Smiling, Eric came through the little gate separating the waiting area from the office and walked around the front desk. He knelt. "Well, you must be Ariel."

She responded with face licks, wiggles, and a furious tail wagging.

"She likes me." He smirked.

"She likes everybody, but yeah, she does seem to really like you."

He pulled a treat out of his pocket. "Sit."

Ariel obeyed, stubby tail brushing the floor, eyes fixed on the treat.

"Good girl." He gave it to her and stood, taking the blanket. "She can hang out with me."

"Oh, thanks, Eric." I handed him the rest of her things.

"Come on, girl. Let's get you set up for the day."

Ariel followed Eric behind the counter and he latched the short gate.

I headed to the back but only made it a few steps before the first news crew, camera lights glaring, burst through the front doors.

"Dr. Collins. You are Dr. Collins, aren't you? Can you answer some questions? How long have you had this ability to talk to animals? What have those from the Whedon place told you so far?"

The office manager, Janice Davidson, and Dr. James Whitaker, the owner, rushed from a side hall. Janice took my arm and hurried me to her office.

Ariel barked and Eric picked her up, taking her into the file room.

"Dr. Collins can't talk with you right now." Dr. Whitaker strode forward. "The case she's assisting with is ongoing, and the authorities have requested she not talk to the press. You may call the sheriff's department instead. Please be respectful to our patients and their families and leave. Thank you."

I looked back, hesitating for a moment before going inside. Dr. Whitaker turned from the disappointed news crew and followed us, his expression irritated. *At me?* My throat went dry, my tongue sticking to the roof of my mouth. *Great. Now I'm going to lose my job.* I slipped past the open door and stood in front of Janice's desk. Palms sweating, I bit my lower lip. I listened to Dr. Whitaker's shoe heels snapping on the clean white tile floor and waited.

He swept into the tiny office, the space almost claustrophobic at that point, and in one smooth motion he closed the door and turned to me.

Here it comes.

"Dr. Collins—"

"Sir, I didn't … I mean, I'm not sure—"

"Kallie, please listen. This is *my* fault." He gestured to the chair. "Please." He motioned for Janice to take a seat before he did the same to my right. "I am so sorry we got you into this. You are an excellent doctor—no, *gifted*—and a valued member of our team. I hope what's happening won't create any thoughts of leaving us."

I inhaled through my nose, relief spreading across my humming nerves. "You mean, quitting my job?"

Nodding, he continued. "I realized that when the authorities called several days ago regarding you assisting them, I never talked with you before I agreed. I apologize. If you need time off, just let me or Janice know." He paused and glanced at Janice. She smiled. "We've agreed to put you on administrative leave, with pay, for as long as you need."

Keeping my jaw tight so my mouth wouldn't drop open, I nodded. "Sir,

I'm fine. I'd like to keep working, as long as it doesn't interfere with the care of the patients."

"Good." He stood, smiling. "Then we'll let you get back at it. Thank you, Dr. Collins."

"Thank *you*." He opened the door for me, and I half stumbled out.

Eric and Ariel met me at the junction of the front reception area and the hall to the exam rooms. "You okay?"

"Yeah." I nodded, still trying to take in what had just happened. My attention on Eric again, I came back to the present. "It's all good."

"Excellent. The news crews are gone, and you have a patient waiting."

Bending, I hugged Ariel, a smile stretching my cheeks. "Well, then, I'd better get busy. And you, my little friend, need to keep an eye on Eric."

Chapter 17

My FIRST PATIENT, A FIVE-YEAR-OLD standard poodle named Alexander, trotted into the exam room ahead of a well-dressed older woman. He didn't appear ill or injured. I made eye contact with his owner. Squatting, I scratched behind his silky ears. "What seems to be Alexander's problem today?"

"Well," the woman began, "he's been depressed."

"Okay. Why do you think that is? Have there been any big changes, like a move or a death in the family? Anything?"

The woman tipped her head, her eyes narrowing. "No." She shook her head. "Not that I can think of."

I straightened and pulled a stethoscope from the drawer. I had a bad feeling about where this was going. Back in a crouch, I listened to Alexander's lungs and heart. There was nothing wrong there. "What is he doing?" I duckwalked to another drawer and pulled out a thermometer. Alexander cooperated, and in a few seconds, a normal temperature showed on the small display.

"There's nothing I can pinpoint." She sat on the short bench seat. "I just know something is going on with my baby." A pout formed on her red lips.

Taking a deep breath, she continued. "Maybe you could talk to him? Make sure everything's okay? I want to know he's happy."

Patting Alexander, I stood. "He seems fine to me. I could run some blood tests, but I don't think it's necessary."

"Could you ask him, Dr. Collins? I mean, that's what you do, right?"

"What exactly do you want to know?"

Blushing, she gave me a sideways glance. "Who he likes best—me or my husband."

I nodded and took a deep breath. "Alexander appears to be a happy, healthy dog. He's showing no signs of illness or listlessness, here or at home." I stared at the woman. "Do you think it's fair to Alexander to ask him? Questioning him may really upset him. You don't want to do that, do you?"

"Oh, Dr. Collins. I never thought about that. No, I don't. Never mind. Don't ask him." She gathered his leash, her hand on the doorknob. Glancing back at me as she stepped into the hall, she smiled. "Besides, I already know the answer."

By three, ninety percent of my patients weren't emergencies or even ill. I'd seen two cats, three dogs, a goat, a parrot, an iguana, and a seven-foot python, their owners all wanting me to connect with their beloved pets. Word about what I could do, thanks to the media, had gotten around fast. With every unnecessary appointment, I had a growing alarm that truly sick or injured animals might be overlooked. The security of my job was another concern. My palms would sweat and my pulse would quicken each time I walked into a room.

Coming out of exam two—newborn lambs born with inverted eyelids, a condition easily fixed—I met Dr. Erickson, in the hall. "Hey, Pete. What are you doing here?"

He offered me an embarrassed grin. "Heard about what's going on. Dr. Whitaker asked me to help out."

My stomach did a slow roll. "I'm getting sent home, aren't I?"

His smile widened. "Maybe?" He took me by my shoulders. "Look, it's not your fault and in a few days, it'll all blow over. Turn this situation into a positive. Spend time with your family. Take a trip. Binge-watch TV. Get all your Christmas shopping done two months early. The possibilities are endless." He spread his arms and chuckled.

The *click, click, click* of heels on the tile floor sounded behind me. I didn't need to look to know that Dr. Whitaker was walking toward us. "Thanks, Pete," I whispered.

"Dr. Collins—Kallie."

I turned to face Dr. Whitaker. "Yes, sir."

"Has Dr. Erickson told you? He'll be taking your shifts for the next few days." He glanced down the hall, avoiding my eyes. "Just until things calm down. Should only be a week, or so."

"Remember what I said, Kallie," Pete chimed in. "It's a great time to get all your Christmas shopping done."

I couldn't keep the frown from forming.

"Ookaayy then. See you when you get back." Pete hurried down the hall and disappeared into the employee lounge.

Dr. Whitaker cleared his throat. "We think this is for the best. And things will calm down. Don't worry. You are on administrative leave *with* pay." He reached out and patted my shoulder. "Eric has Ariel's things gathered and he'll help you get them in your car." With a reserved smile, he said, "Thank you for understanding."

He hurried back down the hall and left me standing there, alone in the quiet hallway.

On the drive home, one moment I'd get teary eyed, and then the next I'd fume at circumstances beyond my control. I didn't know whether to scream or cry or both. My emotions were somewhat managed by the time Ariel and I entered the front door, her bed, toys, and a small bag of food balanced on my left arm.

Ella trotted into the entry to meet us. At least she seemed glad we were home.

The young officer on duty was new—well, new to me, but probably to his job, too. I immediately chided myself for being judgmental. I didn't like it when people did the same to me because of how young I looked.

Standing from his chair at the kitchen table, he introduced himself.

Jim something. I didn't really pay attention. Turning away, I dropped the dog bed on the living-room floor and sighed. *This isn't his fault.* Returning to the kitchen, I smiled at Jim. "There's coffee in that cupboard." I pointed. "Cupcakes are in the plastic container in the fridge, and please help yourself."

"Thanks." He sat again at the kitchen table, laptop humming, a notebook and pen on his right. He continued to stare at me. "Bad day?"

"You could say that. With my animal-communication ability broadcast all over southern Oregon, and most of the appointments today being people wanting to *talk* to their pets, I've been put on administrative leave."

"Wow." He nodded. "I wondered why you were back so soon. I was told your shift didn't end until seven."

"Surprise." I held up my hands. "And, really, make yourself at home." Ariel followed me back to my room, where Ella was already curled up on my pillow. I dug into my pack and found my phone. After closing the door, I flopped onto the bed with a bounce, ignoring Ella's glare of annoyance. I texted Sam and Gracie and let them know a little of what was going on. *They* were still at work, and I didn't expect a quick response. A thought swirled in my mind. I sat up, grabbed my pack, and pulled out the paper with the names and addresses of the other victims of R and A. Thinking back on what Pete said about making this time positive, I smiled at Ariel lying next to Ella. "Time for Kinsey to get back on the case."

Chapter 18

IT WAS TOO LATE TO start investigating at that point, so I grabbed a quick shower and headed to my parents—a pre-emptive strike to advise them about my sudden time off. Hearing it from someone else would only make it seem worse. I stayed for dinner—more pro-active attempts on my part to quell Mom's anxiety—ignoring the constant texts from my phone. I figured it was Sam and Gracie and that I'd fill them in on the details later.

What I didn't expect awaiting me at home was a bouquet of flowers along with a small pink box from my favorite bakery. The smile that spread over my face when I read the attached card from Ben made that disaster of a day a lot better. It simply stated, *I'm sorry*.

Ariel raced into the kitchen, wagging her short tail and jumping to get my attention. I knelt and scooped the wiggling dog into my arms. "Hey, you. Are you being a good girl?"

Jim walked in from the living room. "She's been great—a real snuggler."

"Oh, thanks, Jim." I set her down and opened the box. There were four cupcakes inside. I offered him one.

Shaking his head, he held up his hands. "No, thank you. I had two from the container in the fridge. They were awesome, by the way."

"Thank you. I mean, for eating some. I'm nearing overload." I frowned. "I take that back. One can never have too many cupcakes." Inside my pack, my phone blared. "Hi, Gracie. Can you hold a minute? I want to take Ariel for a walk. We can chat while I'm out with her."

"Yes. But hurry. I want to know everything that happened."

I snapped Ariel's leash to her collar, stepped into a cold, foggy night, and closed the door behind me. "Guess what? Ben sent me cupcakes and flowers. *Cupcakes and flowers.*"

"What? Why? I mean, what?"

"He must've heard about work. The attached note was an apology."

"Awww. How sweet is that? So tell me everything."

I told her, not leaving out any details.

"Well, it sounds okay. You aren't in trouble or anything. What are you going to do with all this time off? Christmas shopping?"

"No." I chuckled. "But I am going to look into some of the other properties on Mark's list."

"Without us, Sam and me? I'm working through Thursday, and Sam's on until Wednesday. Can't you wait until we can all go?"

"I'm sure there'll be more to do when we *can* all go. But I want to get started tomorrow."

"Really? After what happened at the Adamses' property? It may not be a good idea for you to go alone."

"I know. I've considered this. I'll just be extra careful."

"Okay. But you need to let us know when and where you're going. And keep your phone on. Actually, you should be talking to one of us the whole time. These are the rules."

"Oh?"

"Yes. No exceptions."

Gracie was just worried, and she had a right to be. I understood that. Sighing, I agreed. "Fine. I'll stick to *your* rules—most of them anyway."

I turned the corner, and headlights washed over the road behind me. I waited for a car to pass, but one never did. I stole a quick peek back. A vehicle, its form hidden in murky fog, kept pace with me about twenty yards away. "Don't hang up, Gracie. There's a car—going slow. I think it's following me."

"How far are you from home?"

"A couple blocks."

"Let me think."

"Hurry."

"Are people out in their yards? Other cars? Anything?"

"Um, no. I don't see anyone. But it's really foggy."

In front of me, the haze parted, swirling. A shape first merged with the dense gray mist and then pushed through.

I stopped, a gasp catching in my throat. "Gracie," I squeaked. "Now someone is on the sidewalk in front of me."

Ariel's low growl escalated to a menacing bark.

"Is that Ariel?"

"Yes." My voice went an octave higher. My heart pounded and I wanted to scream, but I couldn't.

"Ariel. It's just me, Ben." His face cleared out of the fog. "Kallie, you okay?"

My relief at seeing him almost had me on my knees. My breath returned. With my phone still held to my ear and my eyes closed, I called, "Ben hurry."

Trotting over, he stopped. "What's wrong?"

I turned as the once slow-moving truck raced past. Pointing, I stammered, "That, that truck … It, it was following me."

Wrapping his arm around me, Ben whispered, "Let's get you home. You're shaking. Come on. I've got you."

"Ben, is that you? Is Kallie all right?"

"Gracie, I'm okay. Ben's with me. I'll call you later."

"If you don't, I *will* call you. Bye."

With my phone back in my pocket, I grabbed Ben's hand, my fingers trembling.

He hurried me up the sidewalk and to the front porch and pushed the door open. After sitting me at the table, Ben took care of unleashing Ariel.

"You found her," Jim called in a cheerful tone as he walked in. His manner and voice changed in a flash. "What happened?"

"A truck ... followed me ... in the fog."

He glanced at Ben. "Did you see it? Color? Make?"

Shaking his head, Ben brought me a glass of water. "Not really. It raced away once I caught up to her."

Radio in hand, Jim contacted dispatch. "Officer Madsen requesting additional patrols for my location. Standby dispatch." He turned and rushed out the front door, finishing his conversation outside.

Ben glanced at Jim through the kitchen window. "No more walks by yourself at night. No more walking for a while would be best. If you must, someone will be with you from now on." His attention shifted to me. "Promise me, Kallie." He sighed. "It may have been nothing, but until I know for sure, just please be careful."

The door opened, and Jim came back inside. "They're going to increase patrols in this area."

"Good." Ben nodded. "I'll drive around—see if he comes back." Looking at me, he smiled. "I'll let you know if I find out anything."

Silver light collected at the edge of the curtains. Gray mist pressed at the windows like a thick blanket, cold and silent. The fog hadn't lifted from the previous night.

Curled on my spare pillow, Ella cracked one green eye open and yawned. She stretched out her front legs, pulled them back under her, and tucked her nose against her side.

"Fine. Go back to sleep."

Ariel took one glance outside and chuffed, adjusting into a tighter ball.

"You too? Well, I guess that's for the best. After last night, no more unsupervised walks." I pushed curls from my eyes and looked at the clock on my nightstand. "Eight? Really?" Blowing out a breath, I pulled the covers up to my chin. Ben had called at eleven. He'd found nothing, but units would continue driving by through the night. After I'd finished talking to

Gracie and Sam, it was almost twelve thirty. Then I'd watched TV for another hour to wind down—*Murder She Wrote* on Hallmark. Not bad, really, for being up that late.

I showered and got dressed in heavy jeans, a thick green turtleneck sweater, and hiking boots. Grabbing a dark-blue jacket from my closet, I was ready for whatever the day might bring. Now I just had to get past Jim—or whoever had the duty.

Wiggling from ears to stubby tail, Ariel watched from the bed, anticipation dancing in her brown doggy eyes.

"Oh, Ariel. Not now. Later. When I get back." Smiling, I added, "Maybe Ben will go with us." I patted my thigh. "Come on. I'll take you out back."

Sitting at the kitchen table with his laptop open and notebook and pen ready, Jim never questioned where I was going when I fixed a coffee to go and grabbed a granola bar from the cupboard.

Hmmm. Easier than I thought.

In my truck, I opened my pack and dug out the list of the other R and A victims. *"Victims?"* I chuffed. "Yes." I texted Gracie and Sam: *On my way to the Green Springs Hwy. I'll keep my phone on.* I set the GPS, started the engine, and backed out, turning left at the light below my house.

I got four text alerts, probably from Sam and Gracie, before I lost cell service. At least I was above the fog and in weak sunshine filtering through wispy clouds. I shrugged. "I'll reply when I get there—if I can." I straightened my shoulders and watched the road wind into the forests ahead. "No. I'll be able to. It's good." Instead of listening to another alphabet mystery, I opted for *Hank the Cowdog, the Christmas Turkey Disaster*, by John R. Erickson. Those books always get me laughing. About the time little Albert was attempting to rope Pete the cat, a task Hank encouraged, my GPS chimed, "Destination is on the right."

I saw nothing—not even a deer trail snaking through the buck brush. Slowing, I crept farther up what remained of the patchy asphalt. I watched my rearview mirror for cars, but there were none. In fact, I hadn't seen another vehicle for at least the last fifteen minutes. "Very remote." Twenty yards ahead, the sparse asphalt ended and the dirt road narrowed. To the right and through the trees, I made out a rutted, washed-out path just wide enough for a single vehicle. I switched off Hank and headed toward the only right turn in sight, hoping my truck could handle the old trail. It swept into a tight curve, and I stopped a hundred feet in, the main road no longer visible through the dense forest. This path, unlike the well-maintained gravel road leading to the Adamses, had no signs of recent use.

On my left the trees thinned and a shallow canyon appeared through swaying limbs. I continued, bouncing and bumping along, the steering wheel jerking from one side to the other. "It might be faster to walk," I mumbled, jaw tight so I wouldn't bite my tongue. But it wasn't a decision I needed to think about for long. The road ended feet ahead, the tree line blocking what was left of the road. "If you want to call this a road." I stopped and looked at the forest closing in on me. Mist swirled among thick trunks and waving limbs, glowing a pale silver when it reached the rare patches of faint sunlight. I saw no way to turn around. "Great. I'll have to back out of here." I sat there, considering my options and listening to the wind sigh through the tops of tall pines, cedars, and firs.

"Well, do something, Kallie." Without even thinking about it, I grabbed the door handle and pushed, the squeak of old hinges hidden by a sudden gust. I swung myself outside, boots landing in a thick layer of needles. My hair flitted across my face, so I grabbed a scrunchie from the dash and captured the curls in a long ponytail. Hit by the intense scent of the forest—the mingled aroma of trees and musky, damp earth—I took in a deep breath, smiled, and relished the cool, misty wind on my face. A loud, echoing *bang*, followed by three more in quick succession, broke the moment. I froze and determined the direction of the noise—the canyon. It wasn't gunshots. But it wasn't natural either. It seemed mechanical. "Someone *is* out here," I whispered.

I unplugged my phone from the charger and checked cell service. It was sketchy, but at least there was something. Gracie and Sam *had* texted—the general subject the same. *Be careful. Call when you get home. Don't take any chances.* And from Sam, *I've got a bad feeling about this.* I answered that I'd arrived, gave them my coordinates, and silenced the phone. The text took a while to get through, but it did eventually send. That alone made me a little more confident.

Listening to every sound, I stepped to the edge of the trees. I stayed behind a thick trunk and peered toward the bottom of the wide canyon floor, maybe a hundred feet deep. My gaze swept left and then right and stopped. At the side of a rectangular wood-framed building tucked in the shadows of the canyon walls sat two vehicles—a white truck and a dark van. On the far edge, a graveled road wound down the steep embankment. From my position, I couldn't see much—just the building and the all-too-familiar vehicles.

This was no longer a coincidence. R and A had something going on with the properties they stole from decent, well-meaning people. *But what?* "It has to be drugs, but—"

Bang. Bang. Bang. From inside the building, the sound echoed off the canyon walls. The thrum of a generator cycling on chugged on the far side of the structure.

"Okay. They're building something." I glanced behind and around me and then back down the canyon. "But what?"

Two men emerged carrying a shiny metal cylinder the size of those large thermoses they have at football games.

"Something liquid?"

The men lifted the container into the bed of the truck. Hands on hips, they looked toward the forest on my side of the canyon.

I stepped into the shadows and shifting limbs, my back against rough bark. "They didn't see me. They couldn't have." My tone was that of a whispered prayer. Looking at my dark clothing, I chuckled. "At least I dressed for the mission." With slow movements, I peeked around the tree. The men leaned against the rear side panel of the truck, staring at the serpentine gravel road.

"Waiting. For what? Or who?"

A gust raced from the far side, carrying the low rumble of an engine in my direction. An approaching vehicle flashed through swaying branches in the forest above. A silver Jeep snaked a slow path, settling out of sight behind the building. The two men pushed off the truck and disappeared, joining the new arrival. With a quick expiratory wheeze and a pop, the generator stopped.

Stepping deeper into the woods to my right, I tried to get a better visual at what I assumed was the front of the building. A hundred feet farther along, I reached a copse of cedars, and a clear line of sight to the front. Another barn-type door with two parts that slid in opposite directions on top runners was closed. If they'd been open, I wouldn't have seen much anyway. "Too far away. Binoculars would be handy. Note—pack binoculars for next time." Patting my pocket, I freed my phone. "Maybe some pictures would help." I checked the time. It was eleven thirty. I sat cross-legged on a cushion of cedar boughs, making sure I had a good view through the low branches. I didn't have to wait long.

The previous two men carried out another cylinder, set it in the bed, and closed the tailgate.

I snapped off a series of photos, the image magnified. "Okay. You're loaded and ready to go." Not in any position to follow them, I sighed. "Where are you going from here? The Adamses' property? Or does it come from there to this location? Are these disbursement sites or some kind of assembly line?" I scooted forward a few inches, holding a branch to steady the constant swaying, and leaned in for a better view. The third person came out the doors, pulled them closed, and adjusted a chain and padlock.

I snapped several pictures—more of the three men, vehicles, and the shiny metal containers in the bed of the white truck.

All three strode to their vehicles and made their way up the winding gravel road. I took more shots, hoping for clear views of their license plates. The low thrum of engines faded soon after the truck, van, and Jeep disappeared into the trees. "I wonder where that road comes out."

I sat there listening to the wind whistling in the trees and watched dark clouds race across what was left of the fading blue sky. A sudden gust brought the fresh scent of rain, and an icy chill spider-walked up my spine. I shivered and zipped my coat closed.

"They won't be back anytime soon." I nodded and scanned the canyon walls, my gaze stopping at a downed tree that almost reached the rock-strewn floor. I stood up and trudged through low brush to the exposed root of the poor tree. Limbs, some broken and others bent, stood out like rungs on a ladder. I'd found a way down and back up again. With my phone tucked in a zipped pocket, I climbed up and bounced a few times, check-ing the fallen tree's stability. There wasn't so much as a creak. "So, Kallie, what are you going to do? You promised Gracie and Sam you'd be careful and not take any chances." I stared at the wooden structure, a mere two hundred yards away, taunting and beckoning me. Taking a deep breath, I made my decision and scurried down the trunk, swinging from one branch to the next like Dr. Grant and Tim in *Jurassic Park*. *Sheesh. I do watch way too much TV.* Panting, I reached the bottom and jumped the last two feet to the ground.

I ducked behind what remained of the tree's top hanging branches and listened for the growl of engines, the crunch of tires on gravel, or the idle whistling of a watchman. Nothing. After checking the eaves for any sur-veillance devices or trail cams and seeing none, I raced across the rocky ground to the front. I listened and again heard nothing but the roaring wind so I jiggled the chain held by the padlock. "Note—also bring a lock pick or bolt cutters." The high chuckle that bubbled out of my throat was near hysteria. I inhaled and willed the butterflies in my stomach to calm down. "Right."

I edged around the structure, still seeing no cameras. I glanced toward the top of the gravel road. There was no gate—not even a no-trespassing sign. "They must think being this remote is protection enough. And without gates and signs, they aren't calling any attention to the property. There's no one out here to get curious and snoop round—except me." I giggled, the unmelodious chortle one octave below panic but rapidly approaching terror.

My attention back on the building, I focused my nervous energy. The generator stood silent below the only window, a grimy three-foot square. With my back pressed to the wall, I sidestepped to it and peered in. The glare off the glass made seeing inside difficult. I turned and pressed against the still-warm side of the generator, cupping my hands to the window and my face.

Two tables took shape in the dim space. There were no cots with rolled-up sleeping bags, no chairs—nothing that would indicate any full- or even part-time inhabitant. More shoe-size boxes were scattered over the dirt floor. A dozen shiny cylinders lined the back wall, their metal tops hanging from the handles with twine. My eyes adjusted to the gloomy interior. Two heavy hammers—no, rubber mallets—lay on each table. "Bang, bang, bang," I whispered, my breath fogging the window. Attempts at photographing the inside showed only a bright glare, but I did take a few of the generator and the exterior of the building.

The first cold drops of rain landed with a soft *phifft*.

My thoughts circled around backing my truck down a muddy, slick road of ruts without getting stuck. "Okay. Yeah. Time to go." I retraced my path. A powerful gust rattled the doors and released a quick whiff of an astringent chemical odor as I came around the corner. I covered my nose and mouth but stopped at the outer edge of the closest door. Pulling with my free hand, I managed to pry the door from the side of the building about an inch before the bottom hung up on rocky, uneven ground. Still covering my mouth and pinching my nose, I peeked inside. There was nothing I hadn't seen from the window, except that a small liquid puddle, the size of a baseball shimmered white on the dirt just inside where the two doors met. Releasing the door, I stepped forward and searched the ground. Another quarter-size drop glimmered at my feet. "I'm not touching that," I said, my voice nasal and muted behind my hand. I patted my pockets and found a handful of Kleenex and an empty peanut M&M's wrapper. I dabbed at the goo, careful not to get any on my skin, wrapped it in another tissue, and stuffed it in the candy wrapper. An odd relief swept over me. "I'll figure out where to take the goo later and get it analyzed. It could be proof." I frowned. "Note—exam gloves and specimen cups."

I rushed back to the fallen tree, grabbed a low branch, swung my legs to the trunk, and scrambled up. At the top, I jumped off the root ball and into the safety of concealing shadows. The rain tapped on cedar boughs, and wind gusts drove the drops sideways.

I hurried to my truck while wiping the pitch from my hands onto my pants. It didn't help. My fingers still stuck together. I glanced around for a patch of dry dirt, which is what we used as kids. We weren't sure it was the best thing to do, but it stopped the stickiness. I didn't see any patches around me, though. With my fingers still sticky, I shut myself inside the cab just as the rain began to assault the forest canopy in earnest. I backed up, dodging the trees and bouncing out of ruts. Sliding onto the gravel road, I headed toward the freeway—and cell service. "Okay. Time to call Ben. What are you going to say? Hey, Ben. I found two barns with tables and small boxes in remote properties that have ties to R and A. Drug dealers, right?" I considered the laws regarding empty boxes. "Hmmm. Nope. But wait. There's more. I'm pretty sure R and A stole the land from people who didn't understand what they were signing. And, no, I can't prove it—not yet, anyway."

Ten minutes later, side roads with houses set back on the land appeared. I relaxed my sticky hold on the steering wheel and exhaled a long breath, not realizing until then how spooked I'd been out there alone.

Maybe this wasn't such a good idea. I'd hear plenty from Gracie and Sam when I told them what I'd found—and about my plan to return that night. I wanted some answers, and the only way I'd get them was if I dug deeper. "They'll understand. They met John and Eva Adams. Besides, it's better to tell them than Ben." I grimaced. "At least for now. We just need more proof before talking to the authorities."

Chapter 19

MY STOMACH GROWLED BEFORE I reached town. I patted the emptiness. "It *is* after one." I turned into a drive-through, ordered, got back on the freeway, and headed home. Thoughts spinning, I wanted to write this all down, make plans, and call Gracie and Sam.

Back on duty, Craig stood in the kitchen, a small ice chest on the counter. He pulled a sandwich and a soda from it. "Hi, Doc. I let Ariel out back. Hope that's okay."

"Yeah, that's great. Thank you. I have some work to do, so just make yourself at home." I handed him the TV remote, hoping I hadn't gotten any pitch on it, and smiled. "Thank you, really. I mean it."

"No problem, Doc." He smiled and held up the remote. "And thank you."

I let Ariel in, who was frantic by that time, yowling and pawing at the patio doors. Taking lunch to my room, I stopped at my office and grabbed a notebook and pen.

Ella yawned and glanced in my direction before resuming her nap on what was clearly *her* side of the bed on *her* pillow.

In my bathroom, I washed with lots of warm soapy water, getting as much stickiness off as I could. It would take at least one more scrubbing. "Note—next time, wear work gloves."

I walked around the bed, dropped my pack on the floor, and put my lunch on the nightstand. After adjusting my pillows, I sat against the headboard. Ariel crawled over me trying to get a closer whiff of whatever fast-food heaven was in the bag. "Not for you, little one. I'll get you a treat later. First, I have to get this all down while it's fresh in my mind."

Ariel gave up and settled in with her back to my legs, sighing with a suffering emphasis.

I opened the pad. Starting with the most recent property, I wrote down every detail—the rutted old path, the downed tree, what I'd seen inside the barn, the photos I'd taken, and, most important, the shiny gooey sample of stuff in the glovebox of my truck. I continued with the Adamses' property between bites of a warm burrito and sips of icy-cold Dr. Pepper.

Clouds slipped down the mountain and into town with a whisper. Once settled, fat drops pummeled roofs and slapped against windows. Intermittent gusts moaned under the eaves and broke up the constant drum of rain.

I turned on the lamp and rummaged in my pack for the phone. After tapping out a message for Sam and Gracie, I hit send. Since I didn't expect a response for a while, I lay down, just to rest.

Jerked awake by a vibrating noise followed by my not-so-quiet ringtone, it took me a minute to compute where I was and what woke me. I grabbed my phone. It was Gracie. "Hey. Hi. Didn't think I'd hear from you so soon."

"It's four thirty."

"What?" I sat up, swung my feet to the floor, and glanced at the clock. *Unbelievable.*

"Were you asleep? I'm sorry I woke you."

"No, that's okay. I guess my outing this morning took more out of me than I thought."

"Exactly. What did you find?"

"A lot. I can't wait to tell you and Sam. When does she get off?"

"Not until seven."

"Gracie, I want to go back out there tonight. We can drive in without anyone—"

"'We'? Wait a minute, Kallie. Hiking around during the day is one thing. But in the dark?"

"We can do this. I have it all figured out. They'll never know." She didn't respond. "You still there?"

"Yeah."

"Right now, we have nothing to prove that R and A has done anything wrong, even though we know they have. Something is going on at these properties, and it's not good. We need proof."

"You're right. It's not good. You've got cops living in your house to protect you. People have disappeared. At least one was murdered. Don't you think it's time to tell Ben what we know and let him handle it?"

"I guess so. But just look at what I've got before deciding. Okay?"

"Okay. I'll be right over. No use freaking Sam out with all this—not yet, anyway."

"Great. I'll make grilled cheese." My tone melodic, I sang, "And there's cupcakes."

"I said I'm coming." Gracie paused. "Um, what kind of cupcakes?"

I made the sandwiches and prepared two plates of apple slices, celery sticks, baby carrots, and broccoli with dip. I invited Craig to join us, and he did. After dinner, I set out the five cupcakes from the fridge, along with the four from Ben—a veritable feast.

"Thanks, Doc. I love grilled cheese. Great on a rainy night." Craig retired to the living room, remote in hand, and settled into the recliner.

Watching him, Gracie nodded. "I like him."

"Me too. He kinda reminds me of a younger version of my dad." I picked up the leftover fruit and veggies, wrapped them up, and set the plates in the fridge, thinking Sam would want to eat when she got there.

Gracie and I moved into the dining room, and I handed her my notes.

Settling at the table, she started reading.

Ariel whined at the patio doors.

"You sure? It's wet and cold out there." I turned on the porch light and watched her race into the back.

Wind whipped the rain inside.

Ariel took care of business and flew in through the open door before I had a chance to close it.

"That was quick. Good girl."

I sat next to Gracie and waited while she read, ready to answer any questions.

After turning the last page, Gracie put her hands on the table and stared at me. Her voice low, she asked, "You climbed down a tree?"

The doorbell rang.

"I got it," Craig called. "It's Sam," he said a moment later, poking his head around the corner. He frowned at the papers on the table but didn't say anything.

"Thanks." Sam swept into the room, dropped her bag on the floor, and sat down. She glared at Gracie and me. "What happened today?"

I motioned for Gracie to pass Sam my notes. "I'll fix you something to eat."

"I'll help." Gracie slid the pages to her. "You read."

Absorbed in the task Gracie gave her, Sam bent over the notes.

I finished cooking and set the grilled cheese in front of Sam.

Sitting back and staring at me, she said, "You climbed a tree?"

"Shhhh." I held a finger to my lips and glanced over my shoulder. "It wasn't that bad. The tree was more at an angle, so, no, not really." I leaned over the table. "Look. The whole building was new—wooden walls, metal roof, the generator ... The two are almost identical."

"Except for the metal cylinders." Gracie drummed her fingers on the table.

"And the heavy mallets," Sam added, her nose wrinkling.

"Wait, and there wasn't a generator at the Adamses'." I pulled the pages toward me and scribbled a note in the margins.

"What's this?" Sam pointed at the squiggling lines of a poorly drawn map.

"Oh. That's how to get to the downed tree. I was kinda thinking ...

maybe we could, you know, go check out the inside of the building, uh, tonight."

"What?" Sam bellowed.

Gracie and I both grabbed her arms and made shushing noises.

"You ladies okay in there?"

"We're fine. All good." I frowned at Sam and lowered my voice. "It's just a thought."

"A bad one. I can't believe you'd even think about something like that." Sam switched her glare from me to Gracie. "And you. I assumed you'd know better."

Her hands in the air, Gracie sat back. "I know it's a bad idea. I was trying to talk her out of it."

The doorbell chimed.

"I got it."

We heard male voices in the entryway.

Shrugging, I glanced toward the kitchen. "More cops?"

Ben came in with a guarded expression, his hands in the pockets of his heavy jacket.

"Ben?" I pushed the papers away and stood.

Sam's head jerked up from her sandwich, her voice muffled with a mouthful of toasty sourdough bread and melty cheese. "Ben?"

"Hi, Ben," Gracie called. She shuffled the papers, tidied them, and set the pile to her side.

"Want grilled cheese?" I said as I smiled, too toothy, too eager.

He sat down. "Sure. Sounds good. Thanks."

Rushing to the kitchen, I mouthed at Sam and Gracie, "Do something."

Sam pushed the plates of fruit and veggies to him. "Here. Start with this."

"I'd rather start with those." He pointed to the stack of papers next to Gracie.

"Oh. Well. Um." Gracie looked at me, her eyes wide. "Kallie?"

Spatula in hand, I nodded. "We were going to let him see anyway. Go ahead."

Craig edged around the entry into the kitchen and shrugged. "Sorry, Doc. I knew something was up, and, well, Ben told me enough about what was going on with R and A and other things. I just felt I needed to let him know."

I smiled. "It's okay. Like I said, we were going to turn everything over to him." My shoulders slumped. "At some point."

Ben nodded at Craig and then looked at me. "I had a feeling that once you didn't have work to occupy your curiosity, I'd have to watch that Kinsey side of you." After skimming the pages, Ben looked at me. "You climbed a tree?"

"What is it with the tree?" I scooped the sandwich from the pan and transferred it to a plate, cheese dripping over the edges of the golden-brown bread. "Is that all you're getting from my notes?"

Ben took the plate and thumbed through the pages again. He took a pen from his pocket and started making his own notes. With his other hand, he took a bite of the sandwich. "Whoa, this is good."

"Don't sound so surprised. Grilled cheese is kinda hard to mess up." I grinned at him. "What would you like to drink?"

Wiping his mouth with a napkin, Ben shifted his gaze back to the papers. "Pepsi?" He glanced at Craig. "Have you seen this?" Motioning him over, Sam gave up her chair so Craig could be next to Ben, and then she settled in by Gracie.

"Should I make coffee?"

Passing another page to Craig, Ben grimaced. "That would be great." His eyes stayed on mine. "Thanks, Kallie."

"Hi, Ben. I'm Sam." She waved, getting his attention.

"Nice to meet you, Sam. I hear you're the only one trying to keep this one—he tossed his head in my direction—"out of trouble."

"Hey," Gracie grumbled. "I was totally talking her out of tonight's adventure."

"'Tonight's'?" Eyes narrowed, Ben stared at me.

Craig leaned back in his chair with his arms crossed and frowned at me. "Doc. Really?"

"I was only, you know, throwing it out there." I fumbled with the coffee pods. "For feedback."

Tapping his pen, Ben asked, "So these notes like 'next time bring binoculars,' or gloves or—oh, and this is my favorite—a lockpick or bolt cutters weren't part of a plan to return?"

"The gloves were to keep the pitch off my hands—from the tree." Biting my lip, I frowned. Wanting to get the focus off me, and the tree, I changed the subject. "Speaking of looking into things, who was the detective that checked on R and A at the planning department a few months ago?" I inhaled. "And who did they talk to?"

Chuckling, Craig shook his head. "I see what you mean, Ben."

"What?" I glanced at Craig. "This seems important. I mean, I'm not blaming anyone, but I think someone, maybe from planning, didn't check into the detective's questions. If they had, they would have found the same things we did."

Craig squinted. "Which are?"

Peeking at Sam, I asked, "Is it okay? Can I show him?"

She shrugged and nodded. "Sure. Just remember what Mark said. If anyone asks, he had nothing to do with this."

"Sam's cousin, Mark, works in the planning department. He saw a pattern. Things happened that he knew were shady. And he tried to tell people. No one listened to him." Through my rant, I took his notes from my pack, along with what we had found on the internet, and handed them to Ben.

Frowning, he just passed them to Craig, who set them on top of the others.

"Oh, and thanks for the cupcakes and flowers." I handed the plate of treats to Ben. "I'm sorry I didn't thank you last night."

"Aww, that was so sweet, Ben." Sam almost melted in her chair.

"You're welcome. And I am sorry you were put on leave. We don't know who keeps leaking it to the press. I'm still looking into—What flowers?"

That first tiny jolt of electricity tingled at the nape of my neck. "The ones that arrived with the cupcakes."

"I only sent cupcakes."

My head swiveled to the vase with pink, yellow, and white carnations. "Those," I whispered.

Setting his sandwich down, Ben stood and moved to the kitchen island.

He inspected the carnations, the baby's-breath, and the dark green ferns for a card. "Nothing."

"I'll check florists tomorrow—find out where they came from, and from whom." Craig made notes in a small pad. "Probably nothing." He glanced at me. "Maybe from your work?"

"Maybe. Not sure. I—"

Sam gasped. "Kallie. Check your notes. Is the name of the delivery company that delivered, or swapped, the checks in R and A's land scam listed?"

Gracie pulled the stack toward her and looked through the notes from Mark. She shook her head. "Just that each recipient of a check from a title company requested the same service."

"Would Mark know? Or be able to get that information?" I glanced at Sam.

"What delivery service? What checks from what title companies?" Ben glared around the table at us. His piercing stare stopped on me.

I pointed at the papers he'd handed off to Craig. "It's all there."

This time, Ben took a moment to read them, giving them to Craig as he finished.

The coffee was ready, so I set out cups, sugar, and cream and waited for Ben and Craig to finish.

I dropped into a chair. "It's nothing. Or not enough. Right?"

"No. It's something. I'm sorry I didn't pay attention to what you were saying, Kallie. We will look into this further. I promise." Ben glanced at Craig. "What do you think?"

"This is definitely something, Doc." Craig sighed. Eyes narrowing, he stared over at Ben. "And the first place I'd start is just like the doc said— who the detective was and who they talked to in planning." He leaned forward and lowered his voice. "May take you places you don't want to go, Ben."

Focused on the papers, Ben nodded. "Yeah. I know." He peered at me. "And where is this goo stuff you found?"

"Oh, still in my truck." I scowled. "Didn't want it in the house."

"Good idea. I'll take it with me when I leave." His brow furrowed. "What about all the pictures you took?"

"They didn't really turn out. Can't see numbers or faces. I was too far away." I pulled them up on my phone and handed it to him.

Swiping through them, he nodded. "Can you forward them to me? I'll see what our forensic techs can do." He sat there, sipping his Pepsi and tapping one finger on the table. "Kallie. Have you talked to the cat yet?"

Staring at an empty plate, I frowned and bit at my lip. "No. I guess I didn't think about it, but—" I shifted my attention to Ben and then looked around the table. "Help yourself. I'll be right back."

Chapter 20

ELLA SAT ON THE FOOT of my bed, waiting and ready, as if she knew. Well, she probably did. With everything going on, all the emotions and feelings, how could she not?

"Hey, kitty girl. Feel like having a chat?" I sat down next to her and scratched behind her soft ears.

A low whine followed a snuffle at my closed bedroom door.

"Should I let Ariel in?"

Watching the door, Ella yawned.

"I'll say that's a yes." I let Ariel in and she made herself comfortable on the pillows. I took a deep breath and closed my eyes, trying to empty distractions from my mind. I pictured Ella and Ariel under the house, watching the two men drag another man across the yard and through the gate. I remembered Ariel showing Ella retreating farther. I tried to rewind the vision to before the two frightened friends hid. The images that came from Ella were not at all what I'd expected.

Ella left Ariel, slipped through a hole in the deck skirting, and raced across the gravel drive into the low tangle of brush. Working her way around, she crouched on the far side of the small clearing, watching.

Mr. Smith (I recognized him from the R and A picture), red faced, sweating, and panting helped another man drag Mr. Johnson into the clearing.

They let go of Johnson's limp arms, dust settling around the unconscious man.

Ella backed farther under brush and low limbs. The scent of sour sweat and fear crept through the air.

Smith mopped his face and bald head with a handkerchief and stuffed it into a back pocket.

The other man shouted and stabbed a finger toward Smith's chest, making contact.

Anger. More fear.

Johnson jumped up from the ground, faced Smith, and started yelling and pushing him.

The unknown man rummaged a gun from his waist band. His fingers fumbled with the weapon, clumsy and bungling.

Pop. Pop. Pop.

Ella jerked but stayed still and hidden.

Johnson knocked the gun away and turned on him, yelling.

Smith dropped. Blood spread over the front of his shirt.

The other man and Johnson ran back in the direction of the house.

The images faded. Inhaling a shaky breath, I rubbed behind Ella's ears. A slight tremble coursed along her spine. "Thank you, Ella. You are a very brave girl."

Ariel raised her head from the pillow and stared at me, her big brown eyes accusing.

"You're a very brave girl, too, Ariel." My hands shook—no, my whole body did. I exhaled through pursed lips and whispered, "I just witnessed a murder. And I can't *prove* anything. I don't even know the real names of those involved." I walked to the bathroom and splashed cold water on my face. I gripped the counter and stared in the mirror. My reflection was pale. "Think, Kallie. There has to be a way."

A light tap at the door roused me from my thoughts.

My voice cracked. "Yeah. Come in."

Ben's reflection came into view. He watched me, his expression grave.

"You've been in here a long time. You okay?" He shook his head. "Stupid question. What can I do?"

"How long?" I let go and spun around to look at the clock on the night-stand. *Almost an hour.* "Oh." I frowned. "Sorry."

Ella returned to her pillow and kneaded the softness before lying down and curling into a tight ball.

"No. I am. Again, I didn't mean—"

"Can I tell all of you what Ella showed me while it's still fresh in my mind? Before too many of my interpretations cloud what I saw."

Ben nodded. "Of course. If that's what you want."

I chuckled a hoarse semblance of humor, my lips tight and unyielding. "No, but it is what I need to do." I took a deep breath. This time my smile wasn't as stiff or unnatural. "What I *want* is a cupcake. You guys had better saved one for me."

Quiet dropped like a blanket as I walked into the dining room behind Ben, Ariel at my heels.

Everyone stared.

"Relax. I'm fine." I sat between Gracie and Sam and bit at my lip.

Gracie's tone conveyed her concern, her words coming fast. "You are not. I can tell. You're biting your lip."

Ben put a cupcake on a plate and set it in front of me.

Sam removed the wrapper and handed me a fork. "Here. Eat this. It'll help. It's all right. It's chocolate."

"Thanks, Professor Lupin." I chuckled at Sam's *Harry Potter* quote. It *was* one of her favorites. Smiling came easier. "Okay. Um, well, here goes. I saw Mr. Smith get murdered. Shot. Three times. I saw who did it, but I don't know who he is. This man didn't seem comfortable with the gun, like he'd never handled one before." I frowned. "I think Mr. Johnson pretended to be unconscious as Mr. Smith and the other man dragged him out to the clearing. It's like they tricked Mr. Smith to get him to the clearing. That's where he was shot. But …" I stared at the swirls of chocolate icing, "I'm not sure they meant to shoot him." My face hot, I glanced at Ben. "I think the man buried in the ditch was Mr. Smith."

"What about Alexander Whedon?" Ben had a pen out and was making notes.

"Didn't see him—not outside."

"Can you describe this third man?" Craig leaned over the table, his voice soft and encouraging, just like Ben's.

Must be a cop thing. "Uh, no. From Ella's point of view, he was vague. I might know if I saw a picture of him, but now we're getting into that gray area—how much is Ella's vision and what am I adding to fill in the gaps." I straightened. "How are the mini donkey and llama?"

Ben frowned. "They're good. Deputy Lawrence has a small ranch outside Central Point. He's got them there. Why?"

"Ariel asked about them again." I sighed and rubbed my forehead. *Hope I'm not getting a headache.* "I may be able to get more from Ella— just not tonight. It was tough on both of us."

Changing the subject, Ben said, "I think we should check out both properties."

With the first bite of my cupcake, the chocolatey sweetness burst across my tongue, and I did feel better. That low thrum of nerves, icy under my skin, faded and warmed.

Ben glanced at Craig. "How about taking a drive out to Green Springs Highway tomorrow? What's your schedule like?"

"That works for me. Better requisition a four-wheel drive from the motor pool."

Swallowing, I suggested, "Or I could take you." I tilted my head and smiled at Ben.

He held up his hand, as if that would stop my thoughts from going any further. "I don't think that's a good idea. What if something happened?"

"Like what?" I shot back.

"Like people with guns shooting at us, or worse."

"They won't know we're there." My smile grew as I remembered the first day I'd met Ben. "Unless you shoot first."

"It's just a look-see." Craig shrugged. "And the doc does know where both places are."

"We can find them. It's not that difficult." Ben shook his head.

"I won't get in the way. Promise. I'll show you in and sit in the truck if that's what you want."

Ben's eyes shifted to Craig. "When can you go?"

"Jim will be here at ten."

"Good." Ben nodded. "Gives me time in the morning to get a few things we might need."

"Like lockpicks and bolt cutters?" My eyebrows rose.

Ben glared at me with a serious expression. "You can go. But you do what I say. No wandering off on your own. Understood?"

"Yes." I must have looked stricken.

"Kallie." His green eyes sad, Ben slumped in his chair. "I can't be responsible for another ... for anything bad happening to you." His smile seemed a little forced. "Besides, your mom would kill me."

"After me." Sam chuckled, her brown eyes dancing.

"And me," Gracie added while nodding, her brown hair bouncing with the movements.

"See?" Ben motioned to my friends. "You don't want to get me in trouble, do you?"

My smile wavered. I frowned and spoke in a low tone. "I'll do what you ask—honest. And, Ben ... Really. I just want to help."

☯

The next morning, bright sunlight was shining on rain-wet lawns, and a cold breeze toyed with bare tree limbs. I took care of my houseguests. Ariel got a long walk, and Ella ... well, I cleaned her cat box. I filled their bowls with food and fresh water, said a quick hello and goodbye to Jim, locked up the house, and followed Craig to the sheriff's office to meet Ben.

I pulled into a spot next to Craig and didn't see Ben until he jumped out of a full-size, four-wheel-drive SUV at the front of a long line of official vehicles. If the green-and-white paint job wasn't enough to publicize the monster, the eight-inch letters spelling "Sheriff" across both sides was a dead giveaway. Everyone in a ten-mile radius would know we were coming.

I'd cleaned out my truck, a rare event, so the three of us could ride comfortably. I guess Ben had other plans.

"Well? Think this will get us up that dirt road?" Ben beamed, so proud of his choice.

"Yes. But don't you think it's a little much? Um, kinda like a Tyrannosaurus Rex at a petting zoo?"

Craig chuckled beside me.

Ben's smile dropped. "You don't like it?" He looked from me to Craig and then back to me.

"I love it. It's great—if you want to show a powerful presence, but not for sneaking into the woods and trying to be inconspicuous."

"Doc's truck would blend in better, seein' as it's deer season and all. Nobody'd pay much attention to us."

Hands on hips, Ben turned toward the SUV. His shoulders slumped, and he shifted his attention back to us. "Guess I have a lot to learn about the woods and their mysterious ways." He nodded. "Help me get the gear into Kallie's truck."

When we were finished, I handed the keys to Ben and gave him a sly smile. "Might as well look the part. Just one request—coffee."

We zipped into a Dutch Bros before heading away from town and toward Green Springs Highway. When the last houses were five miles behind us and my truck was the only vehicle out there, I concentrated on finding the trail off the main road. I didn't have any trouble locating the rutted path. "There." I pointed. "That's it."

"That's not a road." Ben scowled. He shifted into second and then first, took a deep breath, and turned onto the narrow path, bouncing into the first set of ruts. His head hit the roof, and he almost lost the tug-of-war with the steering wheel.

"Yee-haw," Craig called and gripped the handle above the passenger side door.

Ben stared forward with his teeth gritted. "Sorry. Guess I'm not so good at this off-road stuff."

"You're doing fine." I managed to get the praise out before he slipped into another deep rut and threw us to the left.

"Maybe you should drive now." Ben's eyes darted in my direction. "I don't want to wreck your truck."

"You don't have that much farther." I pointed ahead. "That's the end—there."

"Good." Ben steered to the wall of trees and stopped. After shutting off the engine, he sighed and wiped the sweat from his forehead.

"You did fine." I bit at my lip to contain the chuckle. "Really."

Bands of brilliant sunshine shone through unmoving limbs, lighting up dappled patches of fallen branches and leaves on the ground. Birds called high in the forest canopy, their varied notes clear and bright. The rain-fresh air was fragrant with the scents of cedar, pine, and fir.

Stepping a couple feet from my truck, I listened to the silence and inhaled the heady aroma. I turned at the first slight squeal from the truck's door. "Don't close them. They're not very quiet," I called back at Ben and Craig. "And there's no wind today—not like yesterday."

Frowning, Ben let go of the door. "No wind? Why—"

"Yesterday I had a strong wind blowing from the southwest, from across the canyon and toward this side of the woods. Sound carried my way. No wind today, though. Sounds will carry in all directions." Half smiling, I shrugged. "Best not to make a lot of noise, and those hinges really screech." I held up one hand. "Oh. And you might want to silence your phones."

"Right." Ben nodded and pulled his phone from a jacket pocket.

Craig helped unload a camera with a long telephoto lens and three sets of binoculars.

We trudged a path through wet brush entangled with low branches and pushed dripping limbs away, careful not to let go and slap the person behind.

Edging into the copse of cedars, I pointed toward the building at the bottom of the canyon. "There," I whispered. It seemed deserted—no truck, no van, no silver Jeep. The new metal roof gleamed, reflecting the sunlight. Puddles glistened around the perimeter, and the vertical channels from the gable were still dripping. I listened again. There was no chug of generator, crunch of gravel, or rumble of engine. And no *bang, bang, bang.*

Ben and Craig crept farther, closer to the canyon's edge, holding binoculars to their eyes.

"Pretty quiet. Looks like no one's there." Ben pulled his binoculars away and glanced at me. "What time were you here?"

"Uh, about now." I took a quick look at my watch and nodded. "Maybe a little later."

"May not mean anything—you know, time wise. We don't know what kind of schedule, if any, they're working by." Craig sidestepped and moved a branch to scan the area below.

Turning to the right, Ben pointed. "Is that the tree?"

"Yes. You aren't going down there, are you?"

Craig glanced back at me. "Well, we aren't going to find out anything from up here."

"Now I've got a bad feeling." I slumped, my shoulders sagging.

"We'll be fine." Ben smiled and set the binoculars next to the camera. "Won't need these." He glanced at Craig. "Ready?"

"Let's do this."

I frowned and watched them clamber down the tree. They weren't at all graceful as I'd imagined my own descent. *Did I look that ridiculous when I did it?*

Once on the ground, they raced to the building and flattened against the side.

"Well, at least I did that right," I muttered. I scanned the surrounding forest with the binoculars. "Nothing. Not yet, anyway." I wasn't sure if that first little prickling sensation along my skin was the caffeine kicking in or an ominous foreboding.

Instead of going around the front as I had, they moved toward the back of the structure to the far side, out of sight.

Frowning, I mumbled, "Note—next time head to the back instead." A small electric pulse coursed along my nerves. My stomach tightened followed by a lazy roll. "Hurry up, Ben."

I strained to listen to anything not natural to the forest. I watched the far side of the canyon and waited. And waited some more. Leaning against a tree, I glanced at my watch for the fourth time. From where I stood, I could see the front of the building. No Ben or Craig swept around the corner and into my line of sight. "What's going on, guys? Nothing over there but a generator and a grimy window."

A low thrumming sounded under the high call of birds.

Is that real? Or just my imagination?

It grew louder.

"Real." I held my breath, my heart thumping. Scanning the forest, I shifted my gaze to the gravel road stretching down into the canyon. *Nope. Nothing.*

The sound wavered, cycled, and became intermittently louder.

Can Ben hear it?

I looked farther to the right, beyond the canyon. There it was, a distant shimmer through green boughs—sunlight on metal.

Someone is coming.

No longer a thrum, the unmistakable low rumble of an engine echoed in the woods. It was still a long way off, but it was coming.

Can't Ben hear that?

I hung the binoculars over my shoulder by the strap and grabbed my phone. No signal. I spun in a circle while holding up the screen. I stepped to the left. Nothing. To the right. One bar. I punched in Ben's number. The bar disappeared. "No. No no no." I'd had a signal the day before—not much, but something. My breath caught and my stomach knotted. "Do something, Kallie." I brushed curls from my forehead, my eyes squeezed tight. "Okay. Where did I have it? At the truck? Yes. But here, too." My lids popped open. Moving the phone up and then down, I remembered. "I was sitting." I dropped to the ground. Ben's number rang once and then twice. I held my breath with my arm stiff, not daring to jinx the connection.

"Kallie, we're kinda busy. What's wrong?"

"Someone's coming. Get back here. Hurry," I whispered. I didn't need to whisper—not really. There was just something about the situation that made me want to hide and be silent.

"Copy." Ben clicked off.

I jumped up and pressed against a sturdy tree trunk. Watching the rear of the structure, I waited. There was still no Ben and no Craig.

Reaching down, I grabbed the binoculars. I searched the woods, looking for sunlight reflecting off a white truck or a dark van or a silver Jeep. I thought I saw movement through the trees. My gaze shifted to the building. There was still nothing. "Come on."

My phone vibrated, and I answered. "Where are you?"

"Leaving the building now. Where's our company?"

I scanned the trees. *Leaving the building? How—* A white truck followed by a silver Jeep showed through the branches. In seconds, they'd reach the top of the slope. "Coming from the woods. You need to get behind the building fast, or they'll see you." Movement below caught my peripheral vision. Ben and Craig rounded the corner and stopped, backs flat against the wall. "Okay. Good. Stay."

The truck crowned the hill and started down the curving gravel road. The Jeep waited at the top, exhaust billowing in the cool air.

Had someone seen them?

After the truck parked at the front, two men got out and glanced around. The Jeep started down and pulled in next to the truck. One man exited. Chains rattled against wood. Doors opened with a scrape of rollers on metal.

"Ben has to hear all this racket." Remembering the binoculars in my hand, I raised them, but it was too late. All three men entered the structure before I saw them clearly. I swung around to check on Ben and Craig. They were gone. "Where did they go?" I surveyed the canyon floor but didn't see anything. And my phone had no signal. My pulse beat a frantic tempo in my fingertips. "Okay. Breathe. Stay alert."

There was movement at the front of the barn. The two men walked over, opened the truck's tailgate, and slid stacks of the shoeboxes to the edge.

I watched through the binoculars. "Not shoeboxes. More like white rectangular bakery boxes."

The men carried in four at a time, making five trips each.

"Must be heavy? But not liquid. So where did the goo come from?"

The generator kicked on, the chugging wheeze echoing off the canyon walls.

I kept checking the back of the barn. There was still no sign of Ben or Craig. I lowered the binoculars and looked back down the rutted path. "Okay. I'll give them fifteen more minutes. Then what? Call for backup? No. Just keep watching." I nodded and sat down, hidden among the cedar trees. "They'll show up or call or something. If not, then I'll do something, like call for help."

At thirteen minutes and twenty-two seconds, my phone vibrated. "Where are you? Are you okay?"

"Kallie, we're good. Meet us out at the main road. Hope you don't mind muddy boots in your truck."

"On my way." I gathered our things and stowed them behind the seat. With the generator still echoing a dull *chug, chug, chug*, I didn't worry about squeaking hinges or the growl of the engine. I hurried through ruts, slipping on slick mud, and slid off the path and onto gravel.

Craig dashed out of the woods on the other side of the road followed by Ben. Panting, they scrambled into the truck and buckled their seat belts.

Ben glanced at me with sweat trickling down his cheeks, his eyes dark. "Drive."

Chapter 21

I HAD QUESTIONS. TRYING BUT failing to organize them into some semblance of order, I just gave up. "You were inside? How? You didn't go through the front." Nodding with enthusiasm, I declared, "I was watching." My excitement grew. "What's in there? I mean, besides tables, empty boxes, and those metal cylinders? Oh, and what about—"

"Kallie. Slow down. Let me catch my breath."

Drumming the steering wheel with my thumbs, I waited.

"We got in through the window. It opened out on a hinge and wasn't locked." Ben sighed. "What sort of illegal enterprise doesn't have surveillance of some kind or locking windows?" He shook his head. "I'm not sure, short of how they got the land, that they're doing anything illegal."

"What about Mr. Smith?" I glanced sideways at Ben. "I saw him murdered."

"It still might be regarding the land, not what they're doing at the barn. Maybe he threatened to tell someone about their less-than-truthful dealings with the rightful owners. Or it may have nothing to do with the properties at all."

"So what are they doing there? What was in the boxes? Anything?"

"Not so much as a residue of any kind. I think we expected a white powder, as in drugs, but nope—nothing." Craig wiped sweat from his forehead with the back of his hand.

"They brought in boxes—heavy, by the looks of them. I watched them make several trips."

"Yeah. We saw that, too, through the window. Didn't wait around to watch what they did with them." Ben pulled a small plastic vial from his pocket. "I did get the inside of three empty boxes swabbed before you called to warn us."

"Well, that's good, right?"

Ben shrugged. "We'll see. I didn't have cause to get the sample, so even if it is something illegal, we can't use it against them."

"How did you get to the road?"

"There's a run-off channel cut into the canyon on the other side—just past the barn. That's where we found all the mud." Ben pointed at his boots. "We waited until they went inside and ran until we found a deer trail to climb up and out. From there, we headed in the direction of the road. And, by the way, Craig called it a deer trail. I called it a vertical ascent."

Chuckling, Craig shifted to look at Ben. "You made it just fine."

"So what now? Search warrants?"

The first house set back from the road appeared on the left.

"We don't have enough— No. We don't have *anything* to show for a warrant." Ben let out a breath through pursed lips and glanced at me. "If you're up for it, let's check out the property on Madrone Canyon."

"Um, sure. Good." I fought to contain a growing smile.

❧

I parked on the side path, just like the first time, hidden from the main road.

High thin clouds raced overhead, leaching the intense blue from the sky and obscuring the sunlight. A gentle breeze sighed in the boughs and rattled scarce yellow leaves still clinging on the few oaks scattered among pine and fir.

"Through the trees?" Ben watched me. "Is there a path?"

"We can go up the road." I gestured ahead. "If we hear someone coming, it's easy enough to step into the woods."

"I see what you mean. The gravel's new." Craig surveyed the road. "This wasn't cheap."

"Yeah, that's what I thought." I started to walk up the slight slope. "Whatever they're doing, they must be making money." I glanced at Ben. "I mean, look at Whedon's house and the furnishings. Even the grounds are meticulously maintained, and not by him or his wife."

"Why do you say that? Maybe ..." Ben paused. "Her hands. They were soft—no calluses. Not the hands of someone who worked outside."

"And what about the mini donkey and the llama?" Facing forward, I kept walking and listening. "Were they, I don't know, just for show?" I put a hint of Goofy's voice in mine. "'Look at us. We're country folk. Just starting our little farm. We'll be getting fainting goats next week. Never mind how we got the money.'"

Craig laughed. "You're all right, Doc."

Heat flooded my face. I grimaced and this time didn't turn around, not wanting to see Ben's reaction to my silliness. *Sheesh, Kallie.*

We stayed on the road all the way to the barn.

There were no vehicles out front or anywhere near and no distant rumble of an engine echoing through the forest. Birds chirped and sang on swaying limbs in the surrounding forest. A coyote skirted the tree line beyond the tumbled-down old house.

We walked into the open, no longer hidden by the wall of trees on either side. I stood at the edge of the small meadow, listening to the quiet. It seemed even the birds stopped singing at our arrival.

The coyote froze. Nose in the air, he turned his head in our direction. He crouched, spun, and disappeared under low limbs.

"You scared him." Craig grinned at Ben.

"Was that a, a coyote?"

"Yes." Craig chuckled.

"Is it dangerous?" Ben watched the spot where he'd entered the woods.

"Ask Doc. Then she can ask the coyote." Craig frowned and stared at me. "Do you ever talk to wild animals?"

"I have, yes. They can be chattier than the domestic ones."

"Huh. Who knew?" Craig stared straight ahead, nodded, and set off toward the barn.

Leaving the safety of the nearby woods for the meadow, I wanted to run and get out of sight. Electricity prickled at the back of my neck. Instead of racing to the rear of the barn, I held this irrational alarm in check. I walked behind Ben and managed not to run into him—or over him.

"No surveillance here either—just the chain and padlock." Craig shook it. The lock swung open. "Hmmm. Did they forget something?"

"It's open? Really? Does that mean they're coming back soon?" I tried and failed to control the rise in my voice.

"If you want, I can take you back to the truck."

"No. It's okay. I'm good. That would just waste your time." His green eyes narrowed. I frowned and stepped behind Craig, avoiding Ben's stare. "So are we going in?"

Looking around, Ben asked, "You said there are windows? Where? Let's get a quick look through them first."

"Great." I smiled, my lips twitching at the corners. "They're around back."

Ben stood at one, Craig the other.

"The whole place seems clear from what I can see. The tinted windows don't make it easy." Craig asked, "Can you see any better on that side?"

"Nope. Nothing above a certain point. Windows tinted over here, too." Ben cupped his eyes with both hands and pressed against the lower portion of the glass. "Just dirt floor and the base of board walls. Don't see anything around the doors, though."

I squeezed in beside Ben and stood on tiptoes. Hooking my fingers on the sill to pull myself high enough, I looked through the one-inch clear strip of window. The tables were still there, but not the boxes. "Around the doors?"

Stepping away from the window, Ben nodded. "Yeah. They left the door unlocked. Maybe on purpose. Maybe not. If it was, it's possible they left a surprise for whoever they think's coming."

The image of Data from the movie *The Goonies*, his pockets filled with all kinds of gadgets, flashed in my mind. "A surprise? You mean like a booby trap?"

Craig chuckled. "Yeah. Kinda like that."

"I say we go in." Ben turned toward the far end of the building. "Come on." His hand on my back, he steered me to the other side of the barn. "I want to take a look around."

Falling in step with Ben, Craig mused, "No generator here. Dirt floors at both locations. Whatever they're doing doesn't always require power or a sterile environment." He slowed and glanced around. "No water, either."

"If there's none here or at the other property, where did the gooey stuff come from? They're hauling water? That doesn't seem practical." I stopped. "Mrs. Adams said there used to be a well. She figured it was dry, caved in by now, but what if it isn't? That's definitely a source. They'd have to carry it to the barn, but still ..."

Squinting, Ben scanned the area. "Where would it be?"

"By the old house." Craig set off at a brisk walk, and we followed him toward the heap of collapsed gray boards and rusty tin roofing. Slowing, he angled to the right and stopped next to a much smaller pile of rubble. Bits of rotting wood and pieces of stone surrounded what remained of the crumbling old well. "There's your water." Craig circled around to a spot where only a short stone foundation stood and pointed to a coil of one-inch fire hose attached to the end of a pump. A hard rubber hose was connected to the other end, snaking into a small hole on top of a twelve-inch square box on the ground. "Not exactly up to code." Craig shook his head. "Doubt the water's been tested."

We returned to the barn.

"Let's get a look inside. Code violations still don't give us enough for a warrant." Ben took my arm and stopped me as I turned to follow Craig. "You stay outside when we go in." He smiled. "Don't need to explain to your mom why I had to bail you out on a breaking-and-entering arrest."

"Doesn't mean I can't stand at the door and watch." I grinned.

Craig released the padlock, pulled the chain through, and swung the doors open.

I stood just outside, as promised, and stared in at the empty barn. Bare shelves ran the length of the walls. A faint trace of dust covered the table-tops. There were no cigarette butts, spent matches, or discarded candy wrappers anywhere—nothing to indicate so much as a casual occupancy. "Did they abandon this site?" My voice sounded dull in the vacant space.

Checking the far corner, Craig said, "Don't know. It's possible." He glanced at me. "Maybe they found out someone was snooping around."

"That would explain the open lock. They don't care anymore." Ben pulled his phone from his pocket and stared at the screen. "There's been a bank robbery in Medford." He nodded toward the door. "We need to go, Craig."

Craig patted my shoulder as he passed. "Sorry, Doc."

I dropped the guys off and headed for someplace I could get a burger to go. My stomach growled at the thought of food—a not-so-subtle reminder of how much time had passed since I'd last eaten. A quick check showed it was almost four. *No wonder I'm starving.*

Since Gracie would be off soon, I decided to wait and see if she'd like to get something to eat. I wanted to meet up with Sam, too, but she was on until seven. Maybe we could eat at the hospital. That way I could let both know what had happened, if Sam wasn't slammed.

At five, Gracie and I met at the cafeteria, and I loaded up a tray with a salad, chicken and dumplings, and a Pepsi.

Sam hurried to our table. Her long blond hair was clasped on top of her head, and her blue scrub pants were an inch too short and one size too big. She settled onto a hard plastic chair. "I only have fifteen minutes. It's quiet tonight, but I'm doing an inventory. I want to finish before I leave." She took a carrot from Gracie's salad and bit into it. Crunching, she said, "Come over later. I know I'm going to have questions, and there's no time for answers right now."

I filled them in on what happened at the first place and how Ben and Craig almost got caught. Then I did a quick recap of the Adamses' property.

My friends stared—no, gaped—at me.

Her hazel eyes wide, Gracie muttered, "Whoa."

Shaking her stupor, Sam stood. "Okay. You're coming over. I want details. I'll be home by seven thirty. Bring ice cream—chocolate chip. And chocolate sauce."

Chapter 22

GRACIE AND I ARRIVED AT Sam's with ice cream, chocolate sauce, and a big bag of mini M&M's. With a fire blazing in the hearth and full bowls, we curled up on the couch, ready to discuss the day's events.

Sam licked chocolate from her little finger and asked, "So what's next? You go with Ben and Craig to the other properties and see what's going on at them?"

"I don't know. Nothing for now—at least not the next couple days. Ben's going to be busy investigating the robbery in Medford this afternoon." Stirring, I had the mixture smooth, all chocolaty and dotted with candies.

Gracie pointed her spoon at me. "Okay. Ben's busy, but maybe we could—"

"Wait a minute." I frowned at her. "Last night you told him how you tried to talk me out of going back to the Green Springs property again. Why the change?"

"That was at night." Gracie waved a hand, dismissing her previous objections. "I'm talking about during the day." Her eyes narrowed. "You still have the addresses, don't you?"

"She gave everything to Ben." Sam shook her head before Gracie could ask. "And no way. I'm not asking my cousin for anything else."

"Yeah, I did." I fought back a grin but lost the battle. "But I also might've kinda made copies of the important stuff."

"There's my girl," Gracie cheered and gave me a high five. "Tomorrow's out for me, but Friday 's good."

"Come on, guys. You aren't serious. I mean, it could be dangerous, like Ben said." Sam frowned. "I don't want to see either of you come into my emergency room—or worse."

"I get it, Sam," Gracie said as she nodded. "But we're just going to take a drive in the country."

"No. You're taking a risk going places that might be guarded by people with guns who *will* shoot at you, and big dogs that bite first and don't bother with questions." Sam turned her pained expression on me. "Even if you can talk with animals, Kallie, a trained guard dog will just attack. It's what they do."

"Sam's right." I said. "So far, we've been lucky. We don't know what's out at the other three places." I glanced at Gracie and then Sam. "But I keep seeing John and Eva Adams. They believe they still own the property on Madrone Canyon—the land that once belonged to his great uncle. I know they have memory lapses, but if John had sold the land, I believe he would've remembered." Biting my lower lip and holding back anger, I shook my head. "They were friends with my grandparents. I feel like I should do something."

"You have, Kallie. You shared what you learned with Ben. He knows more because of what we—no, what *you*—have done." Gracie patted my arm. "He's working on this, and so is Craig, and they'll get it straightened out. R and A will pay for what they've done."

"When?" A smirk pinched my lips. "Without proof of some kind, Ben's got nothing. I worry the Adamses won't live to see justice, and I worry about the other victims. Do they even know what's happened to them, or do they feel helpless to fight against it?"

"We should talk to them like we did the Adamses." Sam's eyes narrowed. "Find out what they remember and how it's impacted them. Maybe that's where we'll find the proof Ben needs."

"I agree," Gracie said. "We should talk to the other families. But ..."

"What?" I peered sideways at Gracie.

"Shouldn't we know as much about the land and what it looks like as we can? Then go to them and check our information against theirs?" Gracie paused, staring at the carpet. "I don't know ... it can't hurt to just have a quick look. Could it?"

"You already know what I think. We should see if there are new buildings with locked doors full of shoe-type boxes and rubber mallets on tables." It was my turn to stare at the carpet.

"And you know what I think." Sam focused her gaze on me. "It's not only dangerous, but at what point do you lose Ben's trust by going too far and not listening to his warnings? He's really trying, Kallie. You could get him in trouble, along with yourself."

"I guess I don't see the harm in driving on public roads, and as long as there aren't any no-trespassing signs posted, I'm not doing anything wrong." I took a deep breath and let my shoulders slump. "I do understand what you're saying, Sam. I don't want Ben to get in trouble, and I certainly don't want anything to happen to us. This reminds me of Einstein's quote: 'The world is a dangerous place, not because of those who do evil, but because of those who look on and do nothing.'"

Sam and Gracie stared at me.

"I know. Dramatic. But with all the hate and wrong in the world, I'd like to know I did something, even if it was just helping an old couple find a little justice."

"Wow, Kallie." Sam continued to stare.

"Sam." Gracie turned to her. "Don't you remember—in college, our first year together, our English comp professor? He was bullying those two boys? Kallie stood, walked to his little podium, stared him in the eyes, and demanded he stop. He did and apologized to the boys and the class." Gracie smiled at me. "This is just who our Kallie is."

"Oh yeah. He tried to tell everyone he was just kidding. No one thought he was funny." Sam slumped against the couch cushions. "Maybe it's the chocolate high talking." She sighed. "Okay. Fine. I'll go, if for no other reason than to keep you two out of trouble."

"Yes!" Gracie high-fived a semi-enthusiastic Sam.

"Thanks, you guys. And the minute anything starts to look iffy, we're outta there."

Sam glared. "Promise?"

Crossing my heart and holding up my right hand, I nodded. "Promise."

"Good." Gracie pulled her legs under her to sit cross legged on the couch. "Okay. Like I said, Friday's good for me. How about you, Sam?"

"Friday works, but remember your promise—nothing dangerous."

"If the wind so much as changes direction, we'll leave." Gracie scraped the inside of her bowl for any remaining candy. "So where are we going first?"

"Well, I guess we need a plan." I got up, grabbed my pack from the counter, and returned to the couch. Balancing my bowl on one knee, I dug for the copies I'd made. "Here. The next is out toward Williams." I entered the address into my phone and waited, frowning when the directions flashed onto the screen. "This could be tricky."

Sam sat up straight, an edge in her voice. "Why?"

"Nothing, really. It's actually closer to the California border. Not sure we'll get any cell service out that far."

"Oh. Well, we won't stay long. No sightseeing hikes this time. Just go in, check it out, and leave." Sam's attention darted from Gracie to me. "Okay?"

"Sure." Gracie nodded.

We watched a little Netflix and ate more mini M&M's, and then Gracie and I left.

"Okay," Gracie said once we were back in the car. "What's really going on? The whole this could be tricky, thing." She swept a short strand of dark hair behind one ear. "Your reaction had nothing to do with cell service."

"Well ... I grimaced, "There is the possibility of running into actual drug operations. Because we—the other vets and I—travel around the county, we're notified of areas to be, uh, cautious in. That's all."

"And you don't think this is a problem?" Gracie tilted her head, hazel eyes wide, and stared at me.

"No. I mean, yes, but we're going during the day in a plain vehicle, and we don't look like cops." I smiled and put as much cheer in my voice as possible. "In fact, we'll look totally harmless."

"And how will we accomplish that?"

My smile turned to a frown and I wrinkled my brow. "I don't know. I'm still working that part out."

☙☞

The next morning, I took Ariel for a walk in the fog. We didn't go far, since it was too cold, and I didn't have a sweater for her.

Tara was there when I got back.

"Hi, Tara. Is Jim gone?" I searched the living room and didn't see him.

"Yes. He had classes. And ..." Lips pursed, she stared at the floor. "There won't be any more surveillance shifts after I leave tomorrow."

"Oh. Okay. I understand." My stomach did a little flip.

"Kallie, just because the higher-ups cancelled this detail doesn't mean you shouldn't be careful. I still believe you may be a target. I'll admit I was skeptical at first, about this whole land-scam thing and why anyone would focus on you. It didn't make sense." Her expression hardened. "But not anymore. There's something off about R and A. Ben knows it. I've read his reports." She shrugged. "And about what you do ... Well, I'm starting to believe. Maybe they already know what Ella and Ariel have shown you, or maybe they're just afraid you'll find out. Either way, you need to be careful."

I nodded, the impact of her words catching up. "Wait. What do you mean they might know what Ariel and Ella showed me? How would they know? Unless ..."

Tara stared into my eyes. "Exactly." She moved closer and took my shoulders. "Don't trust anyone."

"But—"

"Not anyone, Kallie."

"Ben?"

"Yeah, he's okay. In my spare time, and without anyone knowing what I was doing, I did some digging." She shook her head. "He's too new to get involved with fishy dealings here—unless he brought something with him from Portland and I didn't see any red flags that'd make me think he's not who he says he is. I think he's a good, honest cop."

My heart squeezed in my tightening chest. "Craig?"

Staring at the floor, she shrugged. "Just be careful. No one knows, but I'm looking into this myself, and it's bigger than just this county." She pulled out a kitchen chair and sat.

I took a seat next to her. "What's going on? I mean, with the properties? Is it drugs?"

"I don't think so—not directly. I'm looking into water and mineral rights, anything worth the risk they're taking. Some have water rights, but nothing worth stealing for. As for mineral rights, who knows? Maybe there's gold but, again, probably not enough and too costly to mine." She looked at me and smiled. "I'm not going to stop digging. R and A's up to something and if people I work with are involved, I'm going to find out."

"There may be people at the county level involved." I took a deep breath and continued. "A friend who works at the planning department said a detective met with an employee there to ask about the properties a few months back. Nothing ever came of that meeting even though, according to my friend, it was obvious something illegal was going on."

"That makes sense. R and A would need someone there to cover up any noticeable errors or omitted information." She raked fingers through her short dark hair. "I just don't get it. To have this many willing to take the risk, there must be a huge payout in the end."

"I've been to two of the places, and they aren't much, other than being rural and off the grid. There has to be more—something I'm not seeing."

"Maybe, but you need to stop looking. You're on your own now, Kallie. Remember, be careful. No evening walks. Keep your doors and windows locked. And don't trust anyone, at least not with everything you know. Hold back a little." Reaching in her pocket, Tara took out a business card and handed it to me. "I've written down all my numbers. Call me anytime."

"Thanks, Tara. And don't worry." I let out a big sigh. "I will."

"Promise?"

"Yes."

My phone buzzed on the table, and I snatched it up before the ringtone began. "Hey, Mom. What's up?"

"Kallie, have you heard from Jeffrey?"

"Jeffrey? Oh, the college professor. No. Why?"

"Oh, no reason. Just curious. He seemed like a nice young man."

"Yeah. He did. Mom? Can I call you back? I'm busy."

"Doing what? You aren't back at work, are you?"

"No. But I'm in the middle of something. Hey, I'd like to take you to lunch if you're free."

"That sounds lovely. How about at that little Italian place in Jacksonville? One o'clock?"

"Great, Mom. See you then." I switched the phone off and covered my eyes with both hands. "It's just a lunch," I muttered.

Tara chuckled. "Moms. Gotta love 'em."

◕◡◕

Not wearing a dress, but not in jeans and a T-shirt either, I arrived early and got a table. I ordered a Dr. Pepper and picked up the menu. They did have hamburgers, but what the heck—I'd get the lasagna.

Mom swooped in at one sharp, dropped into her chair, and panted out a hello.

"What's wrong? You're out of breath."

"I'm fine. I ran into an old friend. We started chatting and I lost track of time."

"You're allowed to be a little late, Mom." I handed her a menu. "Who?"

"What, dear?" The menu trembled in Mom's hands.

"Who was the old friend?"

She avoided eye contact as she waved the question away. "You wouldn't know them—more of an acquaintance than a friend. Just wanting to know about this silly animal-communicating business. I just don't understand why you took such a class, let alone use it." She raised the menu, blocking my stare. "What are you having, Kallie?"

"Oh." Mom didn't approve of the last few days, with a dead body and all the police involvement. It just had her worried. But if what I did helped in the end, she'd understand. "I'm having the lasagna."

"What? Not a hamburger?" Mom's chuckle still sounded a bit shaky. She took a few deep breaths and lowered the menu, staring at me. "Your sister had another checkup."

"Is she okay?"

"She's fine."

"Is the baby?" My voice hitched.

"Everything's fine." Unsuccessful at keeping a grin from spreading across her face, Mom looked out the window.

"What is it?"

"Really, Dani should be the one to tell you. It's her surprise." Mom's grin burst into a full-on smile.

"Surprise?" I scowled at her. This was good news, so what— "She's having twins?" Now I was smiling like a goof.

Mom almost jumped up and down in her seat. She took my hands in hers and squeezed. "Now, if she asks, I didn't tell you." She giggled. "But, yes—boys. They think identical. Please, Kallie. Act surprised when she tells you."

"No problem, Mom. I think I can do that."

Chapter 23

"So that's it?" Grimacing, Gracie stared at me. "No more protection, no surveillance?" She shook her head, her attention on the pancake she was flipping. "Well, you and the fur babies can come stay with me."

"How can they do that to you?" Sam opened the fridge and took out milk, butter, and a bowl of crushed strawberries. "What did Ben say?"

"I haven't talked to him. He's probably busy with all the robberies. News said there was another bank hit yesterday afternoon." I set plates and napkins on the table. "An old homicide just isn't that critical. And thanks, Gracie. But for now, I'm okay here. I don't want to move Ella and Ariel around too much unless it's necessary."

"I still don't see how they can just stop so suddenly," Sam grumbled.

I chuckled while I placed a knife, fork, and spoon on each napkin.

"What?" The word was a chorus sung by Sam and Gracie.

"Okay. What if the body found in Eagle Point isn't Smith's? What if it's older than they think—maybe even an ancient Indian burial? What if Whedon is just a runaway husband, and he finally told his wife where he was? She got mad, trashed the house, and then decided to take the kids and leave. What if the property exchange is just that—nothing hokey or shady going on at all? And what if there's nothing illegal happening on those properties? For all we know, they're making ready-to-bake cookie packages to sell at Christmas."

Gracie brought the full plate to the table and sat down. "Do you really believe that?"

"No." I dropped into a chair and stabbed the top pancake with my fork. "I guess not."

"Eat." Sam pointed at my plate and then Gracie's. "We need to get moving if we're checking out another property today."

Gracie and I stared at her.

"What have you done with our Sam?" Gracie asked, pouring melted butter on her pancakes. She grinned. "I think I like this new, confident, and commanding version."

Sam smiled around a mouthful of berries and swallowed. "Hey, if the police aren't going to get to the bottom of this, we will. It's our Kallie these people are messing with."

I set my fork down and glared at this brave new Sam. "Okay. *Who* are you?" I smiled. "And thanks, Sam."

○●

We took Gracie's car, since I'd used my truck at least twice in these outings, and we'd used Sam's once. Besides, Gracie's had an in-dash GPS.

"It's getting foggy."

I looked up from my phone and out the side window. "Hmmm. I don't think it'll be a problem. In fact, it may be helpful."

"Yeah. We'll be invisible." Gracie snorted.

"Coffee?" Sam pleaded, her hands clasped.

"Yes," I shouted from the back seat.

"Really? You have to ask?" Gracie chuckled and headed into town.

Twenty minutes later, we passed Ruch and toward the little town of Williams. For a short time, the fog cleared, but then we left the sun behind and entered the valleys that wound toward the California border. The GPS led us east on narrow gravel roads, deeper into mist-shrouded forests and back into Jackson County.

"How much farther?" I stretched as far as my seat belt allowed in order to look at the directions on the dash screen.

A soft chime sounded, followed by the "destination is on your right" prompt.

"Good timing." Sam giggled.

"I don't see a road, dirt or otherwise." Gracie stared ahead, searching the trees and brush.

"There." I pointed to the right, my arm between the front seats. "Looks like a turnout. Pull in and we'll take a look around."

"Just to take a *quick* look," Sam cautioned while staring out the passenger window.

"Sure. A quick look," Gracie repeated. She crept into the car-sized notch at the edge of the tree line and turned off the engine.

I unhooked my seat belt, pulled the handle, and pushed the door open.

Sam slid the window down, but only halfway. "Where are you going?"

"I'm going to stand right here, next to the car, and listen for any un-natural sounds."

The window slid the rest of the way down. "I can do that from right here." Sam frowned. "Like what kind of unnatural sounds?"

"Banging, an engine running, or loud voices."

Gracie stepped next to me and hunched into her jacket, her hands tucked deep into her pockets. "Do you think there's anything or anybody out here?"

"Doesn't look like it."

"Okay. Let's go, then," Sam said from the car. Her earlier bravery was failing her.

"In a minute." I squinted through low limbs and dense brush. About ten yards in, the trees thinned, leading into a wide meadow.

The engine of Gracie's car ticked an irregular cadence as it cooled. Other than a gentle wind breathing in the treetops, I heard nothing—no birds chirping and no chatter of squirrels.

Behind me, on the other side of the road, the forest didn't give way to a clearing. There were just darkening shadows and deep branches dancing in the soft breeze.

"Sam?" I leaned over and watched her through the open window. "Can you see the meadow beyond the trees?" I pointed.

Grimacing, Sam nodded.

"Okay. Good. I'm going to walk to the edge. You'll be able to see me the whole time."

Gracie volunteered. "I'm going with you."

The click of a seat belt releasing heralded the opening door. "Well, I'm not staying here by myself." Sam zipped her coat and tugged on gloves. "Let's go—quick." She clapped her hands, the sound dull under thick yarn. "Like a bunny."

Gracie and I laughed.

Recovering before me, Gracie sputtered, "Like a bunny?"

Sam frowned as a blush formed in her cheeks. "Something my grandma used to say." Hands on hips, she turned so she could look at us. "See how rattled you have me? I'm reverting to Grandma's old sayings."

"I think it's cute. 'Cause, you know, bunnies are quick." I snorted, and the giggles started again, Sam included.

Gaining control of my snickering outburst, and my nerves, I stepped away from the car. "Looks like a bit of a path there." I headed toward the slight break in the brush, working my way forward. Stopping while still under the cover of trees, I surveyed the area and guessed the size at about forty acres.

"What are those?" Gracie squinted and shaded her eyes with her hand.

Out from under the dark canopy of trees, the sudden brightness in the clearing had me reaching for my sunglasses even with the fog. "It looks like irrigation?" Lines of freshly turned soil maybe three feet apart ran the length of the meadow. Every two feet, what appeared to be small sprinkler heads popped above the dirt.

"For what? There's nothing but weeds and ..." Sam stepped behind a thick trunk. "Do you think this is a—"

"No." I shook my head. "Not yet."

"You mean marijuana?" Gracie scowled. "But isn't it legal here now?

Why try to hide it way out in the boonies like this? I see grows all over—some right outside town."

I watched the far side of the meadow, my gaze tracking right and then left. "Yes and no. I guess there are permits and lots of other conditions in growing it for sale. Not sure how easy it is to get into the business for recreational and medical marijuana. And it's still a crime as far as the feds are concerned. It can't be transported over state lines either."

"So is that what R and A is doing? Growing on some of the land they conned people out of?" Sam appeared from behind the tree. "Would the money be worth it?"

"I don't know." I shrugged. "Maybe not right away. Not until ..."

"Not until what?" Gracie pressed.

My forehead wrinkled and I bit at my lip. "What if they think the feds are going to loosen up on the whole marijuana thing, and soon? I think having the land and water, and being able to deliver massive amounts of product when the market does open up, would be worth it."

"The three sites we've seen aren't capable of that, are they? I mean, this place is big, but when you think of the demand ..." Gracie sighed. "I don't see it happening on the get-rich scale of things."

Sam's eyes narrowed. "Me either—even if the last two properties are the same size as this or larger. But what if Jackson County isn't the only place? There must be other areas good for growing marijuana."

Tara's conversation from earlier tugged at my mind. "Yeah, but how do we find out if R and A has dealings in other counties and maybe even other states?" I glanced at Gracie and Sam. "We still have nothing to go to the police with. There's no law against putting irrigation on your property."

"But it's not theirs," Sam grumbled.

A chill ran up my spine and tingled at the back of my neck. "Shhh."

Gracie and Sam froze.

Tilting my head, I listened. *Nothing.* I turned in a slow, tight circle. It was quiet, except for the occasional sigh of wind—too quiet. I took a deep breath and closed my eyes. I pictured the meadow and the forest, limbs swaying in the breeze.

Gracie gasped.

I opened my eyes, my mind still in that calm, inviting state.

From the far side, a doe and her fawn trotted along the tree line. Head up, she sniffed the air and then stopped, her big brown eyes settling on the three of us standing across the meadow. She stepped into the clearing and stood still, facing us—no, me. She swung her head to the left, back the way she'd come. She turned to me with dark intense eyes, her message clear. *People, men, laughing, voices, smells, walking slow, working their way forward, strapping small boxes on slim trees.*

A branch cracked in the distance. The connection ended, and the doe and her fawn turned away and disappeared into the trees, two silent wraiths among the shadows.

"We should leave. Right now," I whispered.

"What—?"

I spun around and tugged Gracie's coat sleeve, urging her to get moving. "Remember what I said about things getting iffy? Time to go. Come on."

I didn't have to convince Sam, who led the way.

By the time we broke through the brush at the side of the road, Sam was already strapped into her seat.

Reaching for the handle as Gracie rounded the front of the car, I stopped. "I'll be right back. Get the car turned around."

"Kallie," Gracie shouted. "What are you doing?"

"I want to take a few pictures." I pulled my phone out and ran into the woods.

"Kallie, no. Get back here—now," Sam demanded in a hoarse whisper.

I didn't stop. I just kept heading toward open land. Behind me, the engine whined, followed by the crunch of gravel under tires. Going from the cover of one tree to the next until nothing obstructed my view, I took pictures of every angle of the clearing, getting close-ups of the new irrigation system. Sudden movement on the far side caught my attention.

Four men in camo carrying backpacks and black cases emerged from the forest.

They were the people the doe had shown me. I dropped into a crouch, turned, and duckwalked to the closest tree. With my heart pounding in my ears, I pressed against the rough trunk and listened for shouts of detection from the men. I didn't hear any. I rose, still hunched over, and sidestepped to the next tree. My progress deliberate, I worked my way to the road and paused under low limbs and dense brush every few feet to listen. Again, there was nothing. Relief swept through me, my tight chest unclenching its hold over my lungs. With segments of the road in sight, I started to stand to rush the final steps.

A deep male voice demanded, "What are you two doing out here?"

Dropping back down, I crept to the left and flattened myself to the ground under a fir bough. I adjusted my hood around my face, leaving only my eyes unobstructed, and pulled the strings. With my red hair stuffed out of sight, at least I wouldn't be in stark contrast with the deep greens around me.

Two men, their sidearms holstered in plain view, stood on either side of Gracie's car.

The one next to Gracie rested his hand on the butt of his pistol. "I asked you a question."

Sam dipped her head to stare at the man next to Gracie's window. Her voice steady and strong, she said, "We had a day off and decided to take a drive. If we're on private property, we're sorry, but we didn't see any no-trespassing signs."

"Way to go, Sam," I whispered. "Don't let that big bully intimidate you."

The bully sidestepped and looked at his buddy. This left me a straight line of sight to Gracie.

Both hands gripping the wheel, her gaze drifted toward the woods, her hazel eyes wide.

Making sure the two men weren't looking in my direction, I waved, caught Gracie's attention, and pointed down the road.

Her almost imperceptible nod was all I needed. In stealth mode, I slipped back into the shadows and settled behind a thick tangle of cedar branches.

Low voices came from the meadow, not close enough to make out what they said. On the road, gravel crunched under tires, and the purr of the car's engine faded.

Good. Gracie and Sam are leaving.

I, on the other hand, was stuck there—my back to a tree, under a cover of dense cedar boughs—until the area cleared. My biggest fear was that Gracie or Sam would panic when I didn't show up down the road right away and call Ben.

A limb snapped behind me. My breath caught mid-inhalation. Branches rustled and then stilled.

"You believe they were just out on a drive?"

"No reason not to. They didn't look like cops to me." The bully chuckled. "Besides, they were really scared."

"Should we tell the others?"

"Why? You have a problem with the way I handled it?"

"No. No. It's all good."

"Okay then. Set the camera trap." The bully paused. "Looks like a storm's coming. And we've still got to finish the south perimeter."

Boots shuffled behind me within inches of my hiding spot.

I bit back a gasp, my pulse hammering.

"Not sure the strap's gonna go around this tree."

"Then secure it to a higher limb." A thump against the bark at the far side of the tree rattled branches. "Here. And hurry up. Face it that way. It'll cover some of the road."

Not moving, I glanced up through a four-inch-diameter hole in the boughs. The gloved end of a camo-clad arm swung out of sight. I clamped my eyes shut, barely breathing. After the *zip* of the strap sounded through a buckle, their boots lumbered across dry leaves, away from me. Quiet voices still chattered from the direction of the meadow, just not as close anymore.

No longer able to hold my breath, I inhaled. Blessedly cool air filled my burning lungs. I sat there with my muscles trembling and my heart racing.

A vibration buzzed across my stomach.

No. Not now.

My hand shot inside my pocket, fingers searching for the mute switch. Before I managed to silence it, the first resounding notes of the Imperial March blared through the quiet forest.

Chapter 24

I scrambled from my hiding place. Pushing upright, I didn't think. I ran. Limbs grabbed at me. Bare branches snatched the hood off my head, scratched my cheeks, and caught at my hair. Shadows and overhanging limbs gave way to a cloud-covered sky. Gravel rolled and crunched under my boots as I dashed across the open, narrow road and into the forest on the other side. Trees closed in around me and blocked the light. I didn't stop, my outstretched arms breaking a path through low branches and dense brush. I must have sounded like a herd of elk stampeding in the forest with all the crashing about and snapping of limbs.

Shouts came from behind me, still across the road. I ducked behind a tree, stopped, and listened. My heart pounded out a disjointed rhythm. I tried to breathe without the hitching, gasping heave of air into my aching lungs. *Did they hear my mad dash?*

I couldn't stay here by this tree, but I did need to move with less panic and more stealth. Peeking around the rough tree bark, I looked back. Limbs still swayed from my hasty passage. At least the road wasn't visible, and neither were the men in full camo. It was time for a plan.

To my right, stands of cedars and pines thinned, giving way to buck brush dense enough to hide that stampeding elk herd. That wasn't a good idea, though, since Gracie and Sam were waiting for me down the road to my left. I gauged the distance to the next thick trunk and between several others along a path of escape. I had my plan. Holding my breath, I listened. A jay squawked and scolded from a sturdy limb ten feet above me. I took his call as a warning and crept to the next fir, low branches sweeping the dark soil at my passage. I stopped only long enough to listen for boots crashing through the undergrowth or shouts of discovery. Hearing neither, I kept moving.

Forty yards closer to freedom and feeling confident I'd escaped, I passed two intertwined trees without stopping.

A gloved hand came from the shadows, covered my mouth, and yanked me to the brushy ground. I tried to fight, but an arm and a heavy leg crossed my body and held me motionless.

"Quiet." His husky whisper brushed against my ear.

The bully. I recognized his voice.

"You're lucky I found you instead of my associate." He loosened his grasp so I could breathe again. "Now don't move. Be quiet."

Nodding, I opened my eyes. I glared at him and waited for my chance.

Layers of lacy ferns folded over us, blocking out sky and trees.

An unseen jay chattered and screeched.

The same one from earlier? Did he try to warn me and I didn't listen?

The softest swish of boots on the ground passing just feet away stopped.

Not making a sound, my captor let go of me with one arm. The movement smooth, his free hand snaked to the holster on his hip. The slight *click* of a strap releasing sounded deafening in the sudden quiet.

Confusion mixed with the adrenaline snapping in my brain. My skin felt as though it were on fire, pulse pounding in my fingertips. *His associate? What does that mean? And why is he hiding from his own people? Was this guy part of a rival drug gang? Or worse?* I concentrated on the moment, taking in all I could. *Just make it through the next few seconds—*

I heard that quiet rustle again—moving away.

Okay. No guns blazing. No ricocheting bullets.

My heart banged against my ribs. I took a deep breath and tried to slow the hammering, sure that the wild thumping was loud enough to alert anyone within a ten-yard radius.

After what seemed like hours but was probably only minutes, he took his hand from my mouth. His whisper low, he said, "We still need to be quiet—give him some distance." He snapped the gun back into the holster. "I'm Agent Davis with the DEA, Doctor Collins." He raised his head. "I can show you proof after we get to my truck. My credentials and badge are in a hidden compartment. Until then you'll just have to trust me."

"You're what?" I squeaked. "And you know who I am?"

"The whole DEA team knows. You're the animal-communicating vet that found out more about what's going on with R and A in the last few days than it took us to research in weeks. Like your visit to their office, finding out Smith was missing, the gun found at the Whedon's place, and who actually shot Smith. Doubt we would've found his body so quickly if it wasn't for you. It's made the case against Johnson much stronger. Then there was all the title-company evidence and the confirmation about the employee at the delivery service you dug up." His grimace switched to a smirk. "No matter how many times I tried to scare you off, you didn't stop. Not even a butcher knife through your cupcakes discouraged you." Davis shrugged. "Sorry about that. But you and your two friends almost blew my cover today." He stood, extended his hand, and helped me up. "My contact with the sheriff's department and my supervisor joked about just adding you to the team—figured it'd be faster." He rubbed at the heavy red-brown stubble on his square jaw.

"Sorry. I didn't know—"

"You weren't supposed to. That's the whole idea of undercover." He glanced around. "We need to get out of here. He'll be back."

"Does he know who I am?" I bit at my lip, a frown creasing my forehead.

"Yes. Those on Johnson's land-scam team do, but not the group controlling the business out of the barns." He shook his head, shaggy brown hair poking from under his camo hat. "They weren't running a very sophisticated operation."

"There are two groups?" My frown deepened, brain processing the information and taking a big jump. "Do they know about each other?"

"You are quick, Doctor Collins." His brown eyes narrowed, and he grinned. "And no, Johnson doesn't know about the setup at the other places."

"Does Ben know anything?"

"He does now. After you took Detective Jacobson and Sergeant Blake to the two properties, we knew it was time to bring in all local law enforcement before it got out of hand." Agent Davis paused and listened. Motioning me forward, we hurried away from the road and down through the forest. "I've got a vehicle parked on an old spur road about a mile from here."

Questions spun in my mind, competing to be voiced first. "What's going on at the two barns? Who killed Mr. Smith? Where is Alexander Whedon?"

Agent Davis stopped and looked back at me. He shook his head. "Let's get on the road. And just know I probably won't be able to answer everything."

One mile turned into two, and after almost an hour of hiking in silence through the dense trees and tangled undergrowth, we made it to a narrow dirt road. He stopped while still concealed at the edge of the forest, the road in front of us. With his arm held out to his side, he said, "Stay here." He slipped away, quietly blending into shadows, limbs, and branches.

I knew that standing there made me an easier target, so I sat and covered my head with the hood of my sweatshirt again. Scooting back against an overhang of brush, I didn't feel as exposed. I glanced at my watch and moaned. *Gracie and Sam must be frantic.* I checked for a signal on my phone. Nothing. My stomach growled. I really needed a cupcake. No. A bacon cheeseburger and then a cupcake. Chocolate. With sprinkles. But first I wanted answers.

The low rumble of an engine approached from the left. Agent Davis was in a tiny beat-up old truck, the same truck I'd seen outside my house on two separate occasions. He skidded to a stop and motioned me to get in.

Guess I wasn't hidden as well as I thought. I scrambled out from my cover and opened the door. It didn't squeak, squeal, or protest in any way.

Even if the truck looked like a wreck, it was probably in better shape than mine.

Davis pulled his credentials and badge from a pocket and showed me, and then pointed to the seat-belt clip buried under a stack of clothes. "I don't get passengers very often. Just push that stuff onto the floor."

After I studied his creds, I nodded.

He tucked the case back in his pocket, put the truck in gear, and continued straight ahead.

"The road is behind us—that way." I pointed back.

"We'll have to take a different route." He glanced at me and frowned. "You aren't out of this yet. *We* aren't, that is. I really don't want them seeing me with you."

"What are you going to do?"

"I think I can get you dropped off close to town and make it back without too many questions. I'll just say I thought I was onto something and kept going."

"But I gestured to my friends I'd meet up with them down the road while you were questioning them." I wiped my hand across my forehead. "I should have been there a long time ago."

"Probably not a good plan." The expression crossing his face did little to encourage me. "We should have service in about ten minutes. You can try and contact them."

"What if your friends run across mine again?"

"Yeah." He shifted up a gear. "Okay. Hang on. This is going to get rough."

I kept checking my phone. I'd already been gone almost two hours. "I've got a signal."

"The main road is just ahead." He drove another fifty yards, turned the wheel, and skidded onto the gravel.

Punching in Gracie's number, I waited while it rang.

"Where are you?" Gracie screamed. "Do you know how long it's been?"

"Gracie. Stop talking. Where are you?"

"About fifteen miles down from where we left you, almost to the turnoff to the paved road. Someone followed us out, making sure we left. Didn't think it was a good idea to come back. We kept trying to call you, but you didn't answer."

"Okay. Good. Stay there. I'm on my way."

"Now don't get mad. We didn't know what else to do. Ben's here. We called him. He's with Craig and another officer. They left a few minutes ago to come looking for you."

I glanced at Agent Davis. "Did you hear that?"

He nodded and shifted into another gear. "We've gotta make this quick."

"Kallie, who are you talking to? Who's with you? Are you in trouble?"

"Just stay there. I'll— Gotta go." I stuffed my phone away.

Red and blue lights flashing, a line of vehicles raced up the road.

Agent Davis pulled over, stopped, and turned off the engine.

Three sheriff's SUVs skidded to a stop in front of us. Ben, Craig, and a third officer I didn't know crouched behind open doors, their weapons drawn.

"Driver," Ben shouted. "Keep your hands in sight. Reach through the window and open the door."

"Just do exactly what they tell you." Agent Davis nodded at me and then did as instructed until he was outside and in handcuffs.

Ben ran to my side and yanked the door open. "Are you okay?"

"I'm fine." I scrambled out, looking at Agent Davis. "He's undercover DEA. Well, he was until I ruined everything."

"What?" Ben looked at Craig and the other officer. "Stay here."

Gesturing with a nod, Agent Davis directed Craig to a pocket inside his jacket.

Craig patted the area before reaching in and pulling out a badge and credentials.

I couldn't hear what was said, but in less than a minute, Craig removed the cuffs.

Ben motioned me over and held out his hand. "Give me your phone."

I pulled it out of my pocket but didn't hand it to him. "Why?"

"I think I can fix this," Agent Davis said. "If I tell them I circled back after finding nothing and found the phone in the brush where we first heard it, where your friends were parked, I can make a case that one of them panicked when they heard voices and dropped it." He looked around. "But we have to hurry." He glanced at the three response SUVs, their lights off now. "No offense, but I don't want to be seen with you guys."

I handed Agent Davis my phone. "But if they know me, my name is in the information."

"Already planned for that. You may not want to watch this." He dropped the phone and stomped it with his boot heel. "Oops. Didn't see it among all that undergrowth."

My voice squeaked out a little moan.

Wincing, Craig said, "Sorry, Doc."

I cleared my throat. "No. It's fine. It could've been worse." I looked at Agent Davis. "Thank you. Be careful. And again, I am so sorry."

"It's okay. Like I said, I got a lot of valuable information following your leads. This operation will be over in another day or two because of it. And just because R and A knows who you are, doesn't mean you stopped them from continuing their criminal behavior. They weren't scared of you, just interested—mostly in what you could do. You know ... the animal communication." Agent Davis tipped his head and returned to his truck.

My mind jumped into high gear, and I stared at Ben. "What was R and A doing? And how did the DEA follow my leads?"

"Never mind, Kallie. Let it go." Ben shook his head and turned toward the vehicles. Glancing over his shoulder, he waited for me to follow. "I'll take you into town. Stevens contacted Gracie and Sam. Told them to head home and that you'd talk to them later."

Grateful, but at the same time dreading the hour-long trip to Medford with Ben and a litany of I-told-you-so speeches, I buckled into the front seat.

After ten minutes of Ben not saying anything, I couldn't take it anymore and blurted, "Go ahead. Yell at me. I know I messed up. I should've listened to you."

Ben sighed. "Yes. But you're punishing yourself better than I ever could."

I leaned my head against the cool glass of the window and watched the view outside sail past. "I'm sorry, Ben."

"You're forgiven. Even my boss just shrugged it off. As he said, we did get you involved. And you did help." He stared at me. His green eyes were bright, and a slight grin lifted the corners of his lips. "Just promise me no more Kinsey-type missions. Leave the detective work to me."

"I promise." I sighed and managed a half-hearted smile. With a sudden jolt, I sat up straight, my head filled with questions. "But can you tell me anything? I mean, after all this I'd like to know at least some of what was going on."

Chuckling, Ben turned onto a paved road. "You probably know as much as I do right now. If you can wait a couple more days, we're debriefing with the DEA. I'll tell you what I can."

I connected with Gracie and Sam later that evening.

Sam burst through my door and wrapped me in a tight hug. She let go, glared, and shouted, "What were you thinking? Did you see those guys? Kallie, if I wasn't so glad to see you, I'd … I'd … Well, I don't know what I'd do, but you wouldn't like it." Pushing past me, she continued. "Next time, listen to me." She glanced at Gracie. "Both of you." Dropping her bag on the counter, she fished out her phone. "Pizza? Garlic chicken ranch? And you'd better have ice cream."

"And chocolate sauce," Gracie added.

We ate. I talked. I cried. We laughed. I felt better. Friends. I am so blessed.

Chapter 25

I SPENT THE NEXT DAY with my mom at Dani's house, helping decorate the nursery for twin boys. I didn't say much about what had happened and neither of them asked. The conversation centered on the babies and that was fine with me.

My beaming dad met us in the entry when I dropped Mom off. He held the newspaper toward her. "Look at this, honey."

I read over her shoulder.

DEA CRACKS DOWN ON DRUG RING

With the help of local law enforcement, the DEA broke a year-long investigation into a case of fraud, drugs, transport of drugs, and illegal transfer of properties in southern Oregon and northern California. When our reporter asked lead Agent Michael Davis about the case, he smiled, shrugged, and commented, "Dogs don't lie."

There was more, but I'd read enough. It seemed I'd helped and now the Adamses and all the other families would get their properties back.

Mom looked at me, a tear slipping down her cheek. "That was because of you, wasn't it? 'Dogs don't lie'?"

"Yeah, Mom."

"Oh, Kallie. I'm so sorry." She hugged me, hard. "Can you ever forgive me?"

Dad joined her. "We're so proud of you." He gazed at me with so much love and then grinned. "You know, it's not just grandma's red hair and freckles you inherited." His smile grew. "Remind me to tell you the stories your mom told me about your grandma and some of the exploits she got involved in."

Mom playfully swiped at his arm and laughed. "Don't you dare. You'll only encourage her."

My new phone vibrated, and the ringtone I'd assigned to Ben—the Star Wars Cantina music—echoed against the walls.

Shaking her head, Mom walked toward the kitchen. "I don't know why you insist on those annoying things. Why can't you—?" She stopped, looked back at me, and smiled. "Just turn it down a little. Okay, sweetie?"

I nodded. "I will." I tapped *answer* and walked into the living room. "Hi, Ben."

"Hi. Just want to let you know—"

"I just saw the paper."

"Already?"

"Already."

"Oh. Well. Okay. Do you want to meet for lunch tomorrow? I'll answer your questions, I mean, if I can."

"Sounds good. Where?"

"You pick. I trust your choice, Kallie."

"Oh, Padawan, are you sure?" I chuckled.

"I am. I'll pick you up at one."

"See you then."

෩෩

I took Ben to my favorite seafood place, and we ordered the coconut prawns. Yup, no bacon.

After talking a sip of Pepsi, I asked, "So what was R and A up to?"

"I think you and Tara figured that out. They—Mr. Johnson and, in the beginning Mr. Smith— were buying up property, or scamming people out of it, in hopes that the feds would lighten up on the marijuana laws soon."

Leaning across the table, I whispered, "Did he, Mr. Johnson, have any inside information? Like, is this about to happen?"

Ben shrugged. "DEA said no, but …"

"But?"

He shrugged again. "Now, what was going on at the barns … Well that's another story."

"You're changing the subject." I frowned.

"Do you want to know or not?"

"Yes. Go on."

"Johnson had no idea what was happening." Ben shook his head. "And I don't think he would've been very happy if he had. Some of the crews decided to start a little side business of transporting drugs hidden inside plaster molds."

I glanced out the window. "The shoeboxes … Did they hold the molds?" My attention back on Ben, I watched him.

"Yes and no. They brought the powder in the boxes, mixed it with water, and put the wet plaster back in with a bag of whatever they were shipping that day buried inside. When it hardened, they thought they had the perfect transport medium." He chuckled. "A well-trained dog can smell through almost anything. DEA was onto the scheme right away but let them continue their business, the drugs ending up in the hands of undercover officers all over California and Oregon. DEA's real target was R and A."

I barely had his answer, when more questions formed. "So was it Mr. Smith buried in Eagle Point?"

Ben watched an older couple walk past. "Yes. It was like Ella showed you—a mistake. Rollins, the man with Johnson that day, didn't mean to kill Smith—just scare him. Seems Rollins has gone missing, too. Not sure if he panicked and ran or what. Davis and his team are sure they'll have him in custody soon, or at least know where he is. Everyone else involved in both criminal enterprises is in custody." He nodded. "And according to Davis, they're all talking."

"Alexander Whedon and his family?"

"DEA has them. They've had him since he disappeared last year. He wasn't involved with the scam and started asking questions that would get him hurt. His family knew where he was and stayed in the house so the kids could go to school and have a somewhat normal life until the investigation was over. The DEA felt they should leave after you found the crime scene and gun behind their house." Ben dipped a coconut prawn in pineapple sauce. "He—Whedon—agreed to testify against Smith and Johnson." He glanced at me and grinned. "And, no, that's not their real names, but I think you already figured that out. DEA's involvement is why the department stopped working on the case and dropped the investigation into R and A. We didn't know about Smith until you found out from the receptionist that he hadn't been seen in months. And, oh … By the way, her name is Marie. She's the one that called you at work and left the mysterious note after you'd been to their office. She wanted to tell you it was closing. DEA stepped in and sent her and a friend, an Ernestine Wilson, on a two-week vacation to Hawaii." He grinned, his green eyes bright. "Seems she'd won a trip from some contest."

I chuckled and nodded. "The gossipy one. They should have a great time."

"So who was telling on me to the DEA?"

Ben didn't say anything.

Staring at him, I sat back and nodded. "It was Craig, wasn't it? That's why Tara said what she did about not sharing my information with everyone. Only, she didn't know who Craig was reporting to."

Ben glanced out the window. "This was an undercover operation with only a select few at the sheriff's department knowing all the details. I really can't say any more, Kallie." His attention back on me, he said, "Officer Carter showed great insight during this whole assignment. I wouldn't be surprised if she gets a promotion and an opportunity to take the detective exams."

"Awesome." My frown returned. "Who broke into the Whedons's? And why?"

"That was Johnson looking for Ariel and Ella. He got mad and broke things when he couldn't find them or the family." Ben glanced sideways at

me, a smile lifting his lips. "Guess he doesn't know much about animals."
He took in a deep breath, the humor fading from his face. "Anyway, when
he heard on the news about you and what you could do, he wasn't taking
any chances."

Shivering, I crossed my arms.

"Yeah." Ben nodded. "I'm glad we found them first."

"Speaking of Ariel and Ella, what happens to them now?"

Ben tapped his finger on the table and stared at me. "I was kinda hoping you'd keep them. That way I could visit them. I mean, if that's okay."

"Yes." Heat filled my cheeks and I smiled. "It is. *That way* I can teach
you how to communicate with them."

He reached across the table and shook my hand. "It's a deal." And this
time, the contact was not fleeting.

The End
Well, for now, anyway.

Made in the USA
Monee, IL
23 January 2024

52224968R00111